SWEET BETRAYAL

SWEET BETRAYAL

BY

HELEN BROOKS

MILLS & BOON LIMITED
ETON HOUSE,   18–24 PARADISE ROAD
RICHMOND,   SURREY   TW9 1SR

First published in Great Britain 1993 by Mills & Boon Limited

© Helen Brooks 1993

Australian copyright 1993 Philippine copyright 1993 Large Print edition 1993

ISBN 0 263 13647 7

Set in Times Roman 16 on 18 pt. 16-9312-52891 C

Printed and bound in Great Britain by William Clowes, Beccles, Suffolk.

CHAPTER ONE

'IF THAT crazy animal isn't off my property in the next thirty seconds I'll shoot it!'

Candy couldn't stop a startled gasp escaping her lips as she swung round so sharply that she almost overbalanced off the crumbling stone wall where she had been sitting in the weak March sunshine that had no warmth. The man behind her matched the voice: big, hard and uncompromisingly severe.

'I beg your pardon?' Indignation swamped the fear and her brown eyes narrowed furiously. 'I have every right to be here! Just who do you think —— ?'

'I am?' The tall figure clicked his fingers to his own two black Labradors, who sat immediately by his side like two well trained statues. 'I know who I am; the point is—who are you? And the statement stands: you have exactly four seconds left to call that thing to order.'

She looked from the dark brown, bearded face to the heavy shotgun in his gloved hands and her stomach turned over. He meant it! He really would shoot Jasper.

'Jasper!' Her voice held a note of terror, and immediately Jasper stopped his gambolling to look towards his beloved mistress, leaping up the grassy slope in two bounds and jumping effortlessly over the wall to land by her side, his brown eyes enquiring and his long tongue lolling in its usual ridiculous manner. The two black Labradors didn't even flick an eyelid as he sniffed interestedly in their direction.

She bent to fasten the lead round his neck and he looked up reproachfully as the heavy chain slipped over his golden head. It had been years since he had suffered such an indignity, and in front of two other dogs too!

'Don't you realise that there are sheep about to lamb in that pasture?' The deep, gravelly voice was familiar somehow, but she couldn't place it, and now was not the time to reflect. 'I suppose you're a townie out for the day?' The last was said with such contempt that she reared up furiously with a muttered oath, causing Jasper to growl deep in his throat. He wasn't sure what was happening, but, if there was any defending to do, those two black sentinels had better know he meant business! No one was touching his mistress while he was around.

'I have lived in Downdale all my life, as it happens.' Her voice was shaking with suppressed anger and hurt. 'I know exactly what is in that field and all the others round here. Jasper has been brought up with farm animals and would no more chase a sheep than...' She couldn't think of an appropriate simile and floundered helplessly. 'And we have permission to be on this land!' The last was said with such conviction that the icy blue eyes watching her so coldly narrowed into two chips of glittering glass.

'Really?' His voice was mockingly arrogant. 'I think not. I would have known if I had given permission for someone so obviously irresponsible to walk my fields.'

'They aren't *your* fields!' She pushed back the hood of the heavy, thick duffel coat that was protection against the biting wind that scoured the hillside and immediately her hair was whipped into a mad scramble of tangled red silk. 'They belong to Colonel Strythe and he —— '

'Colonel Strythe is dead.' The statement was completely without feeling.

'I know that,' she snapped back abruptly, furious that this obnoxious stranger could talk about her father's old friend, who had been like a member of her own family, so coldly. 'I was at the funeral last Wednesday, but until they can contact the son the Colonel's old rules apply...' Her voice trailed off in horrified realisation as she stared into the only recognisable feature in that dark, bearded face. His eyes. She should have recognised his eyes! Only Cameron Strythe had eyes that were as piercing as a razor-sharp sword and as cold as ice. She remembered those eyes! How could she have forgotten? And the voice, distinct with its strange, gravelly texture that in the throes of adolescence she had thought so attractive.

'I see I need not introduce myself, but, nevertheless, Cameron Strythe at your service...Miss...?'

She ignored the implied question and stared at him as though he were the devil himself. He was so different! She remembered a tall, smiling young man with the charm of a thousand Irish tongues and fair, clean-shaven skin. This man's face was as dark as an Arab's with long hair bleached almost blond at the ends. He resembled a wild gypsy rather than the cool, university-educated young man she recalled.

'When did you get back?' Her voice was a horrified whisper and immediately lost in the wind as it swirled round them with increasing force, the sunlight racing dark shadows across the valley below. She repeated the question more loudly and he looked at her intently, searching her face with those deadly eyes.

'Do I know you?' Did he know her? She could have laughed if the circumstances had been different. She remembered the last time he had visited the house to see Michelle, her sister. They had been engaged to be married and the wedding date was only weeks away. Candy already had her bridesmaid's dress, a frothy pink creation in tulle and taffeta. The dress was suddenly there before her, clear in detail to the last tiny rosebud on the hem. Her twelve-year-old heart had been thrilled with such finery, but then there had been a terrible scene that night and Cameron had gone away. And later, a few weeks later, Michelle's shape had begun to change too drastically to disguise any more, and six months later Jamie was born. The whole affair had broken Michelle's heart and made her parents old before their time . . . and this man was responsible for all the misery!

'What's the matter?' The perpetrator of all the heartbreak, which had dulled over the passage of time, but was awakened as new as if it had all happened yesterday, took a step towards her, alarmed at the pallor of her face and the wide, staring eyes.

'Get away from me!' It was a snarl of hate and he recognised it as such, stopping in his tracks with an expression of almost comical amazement stretching his chiselled features. 'You aren't fit to be called your father's son.'

As the words registered his expression froze, but she was gone before he could form a reply, running down the hillside on legs that flew over the rough, coarse grass, her long hair streaming behind her like dancing red ribbons, and Jasper bounding by her side, enthralled by the new game.

She didn't stop till she reached home, bursting into the drawing-room, where her parents were sitting in front of a roaring log fire, enjoying a Sunday afternoon snooze with just the cat for company.

'Candy!' Her mother had almost leapt from the chair in her fright. 'What on earth is the matter? You've frightened me half to death!'

'Sorry.' She stood panting in the middle of the room with such a hunted expression on her face that her parents both rose as one and reached her side in the same instant.

'What's the matter?' It was her father speaking now, his voice worried. 'Has there been an accident? Are you all right?'

'I saw him.' She wouldn't have believed she could feel like this about something that had happened so long ago. It must be ten years since that terrible time, and Michelle was happily married now, with two more children to keep Jamie company and a husband who was crazy about her, but every so often she

caught a glimpse of that old haunted expression in her sister's eyes and knew she was
thinking about Cameron Strythe, the man
who had taken her innocence and then let her
down so badly. She didn't know if Michelle
still hated him, but she knew she did, more
than ever!

'Him?' Her father shook her slightly in his
concern. 'Who, for crying out loud?'

'Cameron Strythe.' Her voice was flat now
and she felt the rage seep out of her as the
urge to cry became paramount. 'And he was
so awful about Uncle Charles, Dad; he spoke
as though he didn't care.'

'Perhaps he doesn't.' Her mother sighed
deeply and shook her grey head slowly. 'Ten
years is a long time to be away, Candy; people
change. But it's no concern of ours one way
or the other, is it?'

'How can you say that?' She stared into her
mother's gentle blue eyes in horrified denial.
'After what he did to Michelle?'

'What happened between your sister and
Cameron Strythe was a long time ago and
only they know the real facts,' her father said
stiffly as he left her side and returned to his

chair by the fire. 'It hurt us all, especially Charles, but the past is the past and I don't want old wounds reopened now. Michelle is happy—you know that for yourself—and if Cameron chooses to come back here to live that is his prerogative. He has inherited a vast estate, you know—Uncle Charles was very wealthy.'

'I'm surprised he left it all to him,' Candy said bitterly as she flung her heavy duffel coat, scarf and mittens on a nearby chair, emerging as a slender, tall young woman with a cascade of wavy, silky hair almost to her waist.

'Don't be ridiculous,' her father said sharply. 'Charles loved his son; he was all he had. Don't let old memories sour you, puss; you're too sweet for that.'

'Huh!' She eyed her father balefully as she bent down to remove some tiny sticky balls that had got embedded in Jasper's coat from the dense undergrowth on the hillside. 'That was said tongue in cheek.'

'Maybe.' Her father allowed himself a small smile as he surveyed his volatile younger daughter. 'But Cameron may well be here to stay, and, in a small village like this, open war will make life very difficult for a number of people. You must let the past stay in the past, Candy. I mean it.'

'Dad, I'm a matronly schoolteacher of twenty-two,' she answered drily. 'I think I can decide for myself how I treat Cameron Strythe if I happen to see him again.'

'Oh, you'll see him again.' Her mother's voice was resigned. 'We all will. You might as well get used to the idea. He now owns most of the village, remember, and, like it or not, both your father's job and this house are under his control.'

'Oh, Dad.' She stared, stricken-faced, at her father. As manager of Charles's huge farm, her father had always enjoyed a close friendship with his employer, the two having grown up together, and it had never occurred to her before that their very livelihood was tied up with their relationship with the Strythes. Even her job, as village school-teacher, could be said to rely on 'the big house', as the farm was called in the village. She knew Uncle Charles had kept the school going for years after the council had wanted to close it and transfer the thirty or so pupils to a bigger school a bus ride away.

Her stomach turned over. This was something she had never foreseen, never imagined in her wildest dreams. How could she have been so naïve? Cameron's name had never been mentioned for years, by unspoken consent on the part of all concerned, but she should have realised he would inherit, being the only child of his father. It was an impossible situation to be reliant on him for their very existence, unimaginable!

'I'm going to get changed. Don't forget David is picking us up at six,' she said miserably as she walked slowly from the warm, cheerful room into the colder hall. That was another thing that was grating on her nerves these days. She had known David since she could toddle—all the village children enjoyed close friendships, being such a small community—but lately his feelings for her seemed to have undergone a subtle change which was becoming more obvious each time they met. She liked him—of course she did; everyone liked David—but anything romantic... She grimaced as she sat down at her dressing-table

in her small bedroom, her eyes moving unconsciously to the window and the panoramic
view over the Devon countryside outside that
never ceased to thrill her. When Michelle had
left to get married her parents had offered her
the bigger room, but she had preferred to stay
in her own, where every morning the first
sight that met her eyes was rolling meadows
dotted with grazing cattle, and the faint
outline of gently undulating hills beyond.

Unlike her sister, who had revelled in the
bright lights and longed to escape from what
she considered 'a dead world', Candy had
ached for the sound of ancient church bells
pealing out on a warm summer evening when
she was in London at university, pining for
the atmosphere of serenity and the time-
lessness that the sixteenth-century village offered. Most of the buildings were buff-
washed, nestling beneath the traditional
covering of heavy thatch, from which quaint
little semi-dormer leaded windows emerged.
Now, when she visited Michelle in her smart
town house with all mod cons and the best
that money could buy, the only emotion she
felt was one of faint depression and a sense

of confirmation that she had made the right decision in her own life. She had been offered a couple of prime career moves on leaving university with a first-class degree, but had preferred to come home and take over the village school, enabling the current school-teacher, Mrs Jacobs, to take a long-delayed world cruise with her husband. Mrs Jacobs had made no secret of her desire for Candy to step into her shoes for years.

Altogether life had been good, apart from the irritation of David's growing affection. Until today. When she had met *him*. She gazed vacantly into the dressing-table mirror, blind to the heart-shaped face with its huge, beautiful, heavily lashed eyes and delicately shaped mouth that gazed back at her from the misty reflection.

They were all ready and waiting when David called promptly at six, and the short journey to his parents' home took no more than two minutes in his lovingly nurtured old banger. He seemed a trifle subdued, but that suited Candy, lost as she was in her own thoughts, and her parents were more than capable of keeping the conversation chugging along.

'Mother has invited an old friend of yours, apparently.' David's voice was sheepish as he helped them off with their coats in the hall preparatory to going through to the spacious oak-beamed sitting-room at the back of the house.

'Oh, yes?' Candy was instantly suspicious. Mrs Clarke was the biggest gossip in the village, besides being the most unhappy, restless woman Candy had ever met. She adored intrigue, embroidering the most innocent of happenings in a way that could only be described as malicious, and inventing what was lacking. Her parents knew David's parents on a social level, exchanging dinner invitations like the one tonight now and again, but she could never have termed them friends of the family.

As she stepped through the living-room door and the unmistakable deep, throaty voice met her ears she had the insane impulse to turn and run for a shaming, fleeting moment, before her chin came up and her face set in what her father often called the 'battle zone'. That woman! She had invited Cameron

Strythe here. Just to see the reaction of them all.

'Vivien, Ernest and dear Candice.' Mrs Clarke moved forward in a theatrical pose like an actress in a third-rate movie, her pointed, narrow face alive with hard curiosity. 'How lovely to see you, and I think you know dear Cameron.' She indicated the tall, silent figure behind her with an affected wave of her hand. Candy spared him a fleeting glance and, catching the stunned expression in those blue eyes, assumed correctly that he had had no idea who the dinner guests were either. She also noticed the beard had gone, leaving a faintly paler skin underneath to the rest of the hard, tanned face, and that some time in the afternoon he had had a haircut. The smart, indolent man standing to one side of their little throng was more recognisable as the old Cameron. It made it even easier to hate him.

'He only got back last night,' Mrs Clarke continued into the growing silence, her small black eyes flashing from one to the other in satisfied spite, 'and we couldn't leave him to eat alone on his first day back on English soil, could we?' She gave the tinkling false laugh that always caused Candy's teeth to grate. 'I don't suppose you realised he was home.' The last was said to her mother, who was rooted to the spot just inside the door, and Candy came immediately to her rescue, forcing a light laugh as she took her mother's arm and guided her to an easy-seat near by.

'I met Cameron this afternoon, as it happens.'

'You did?' The harsh voice was quizzical, and as Candy turned to meet his eyes she saw there was a frankly appreciative gleam on his face as he took in her slim, full-breasted figure and heavy fall of silky red hair. 'I obviously was too far away to see you.'

'Not at all.' Her big brown eyes were tight on his face now and no one present could fail to read their expression of cold, unmitigated dislike. 'You threatened to shoot my dog, if you remember.'

The words hung for a moment in the breathless silence that had fallen on the assembled company, and then Mrs Clarke trilled her false laugh into the tense stillness. 'Oh, Candice, you have such a strange sense of humour, always so contrary.'

'You don't believe me?' She shot round on the unfortunate Mrs Clarke as though she had jet-propelled heels. 'Ask him, then. Ask him what he did with his afternoon.'

'That was you?' He stared at the tall, beautifully groomed woman in front of him with something like disbelief on his face. 'But you looked so different...'

'I was muffled from head to foot in a duffel coat, scarf and wellington boots, if you remember,' she said icily, 'but yes, it was me. And yes, that was my dog you threatened to destroy.' Her eyes raked him slowly from head to foot and she allowed a small, contemptuous smile to play round her mouth for a moment. 'You seem to have smartened up a little too.'

He stared at her for a long moment as his face took on the texture of cold granite and his eyes became glacial. 'Well, well.' There was savage derision in the grim voice now. 'So this is little carrot-tops. You sure have changed, sweetheart.'

'You bet your sweet life!' She came back with the retort like a pistol shot, and for a moment their eyes clashed and held in a bitter battle of wills, with neither giving an inch. It was her father who defused the situation, taking Cameron's arm in a light hold as he turned the younger man to face him.

'It's been a long time, Cam.' He spoke the nickname with no false friendliness, merely the unaffected respect he showed to all his fellow human beings, and Candy saw Cameron take a long, deep breath before his body relaxed and a careful smile touched the firm mouth.

'Too long.' He included her mother in his glance, but Candy noticed the cold blue eyes didn't rest on her for a second. 'I was going to give you a call early tomorrow morning. I shall need your help in picking up some of the strings.'

'No problem,' her father returned easily. She stared at him in a mixture of anger and disappointment. Don't talk to him, Dad, she wanted to scream. Hit him and walk out. Her father did neither of these things and there was obvious annoyance on Mrs Clarke's face a few minutes later as she ushered them to the table. She had clearly been hoping for fireworks, Candy reflected bitterly, glancing at

David as she sat down and noticing he studiously avoided catching her eye. Why hadn't he warned them that Cameron was here? He must have known how painful the first meeting would be, especially with a crowd of onlookers. It was a stupid question; she knew the answer. Mummy's little boy would do as he was told. She suddenly realised why his amorous attentions had irritated her so badly. There had been something almost apologetic in their content, holding the same meekness he displayed with his mother. Her decisive, forceful nature had rebelled instinctively.

'And where have you been hiding yourself for the last ten years, Cameron?' Mrs Clarke asked with artificial sweetness as they all began on their prawn cocktails.

'I never hide, Mrs Clarke.' He looked his hostess full in the face as he spoke and there was something in the dark, harsh voice that must have warned her he would stand no nonsense. She flushed hotly and bent to retrieve her napkin, which had fallen on the floor, her thin mouth tight with irritated annoyance.

'Your father told me you worked on the oil-rigs for some time and then bought a farm in

Australia.' Again it was her father who stepped into the breach. 'I understand you were on the way to making your fortune out there?'

'Things went well,' Cameron answered shortly. 'I had some good men working for me.' He obviously had no intention of discussing his private affairs at the dinner table, and Candy had to admit she didn't blame him. She was trying to assimilate the knowledge that her father and Uncle Charles had discussed Cameron now and again, apparently with no animosity. She was beginning to feel she didn't know her father at all.

'What are your plans for the future?' her mother asked quietly, and as Cameron turned to her he smiled his first genuine smile of the evening. Candy felt her heart give a strange little lurch as the cold blue eyes softened and the years seemed to fall away from him. She recalled how often he had taken the time to talk to her when he was courting her sister, often letting her tag along, much to Michelle's disgust, and always referring to her affectionately as 'carrot-tops'. Her hair had been more ginger than red then and she had worn it, much to her parents' horror, in a spiky, short tomboy cut. He had been the only one who had said it suited her and she had never known his eyes be anything but soft when they looked at her, although there had been several occasions, even before the split, when they had been as cold as ice with Michelle. She shook herself mentally. He was a swine and a heartless seducer and all the rest had been a sham. The passage of time had borne that out.

'I'm not sure yet, Vivien.' He let his gaze roam over them all now and Candy fancied it turned glacial as it passed over her red head. 'I shall make some changes; apart from that I haven't had time to consider.'

'Changes?' Her mother sounded anxious, and Candy could have killed him for putting that frown of worry on her mother's face.

'My father was a good man, but too easily persuaded at times.' There was iron in the voice now. 'The school, for instance. From what I've seen of the business accounts a good deal of money seemed to find its way in that direction and with Chitten School a few miles away it seems ridiculous to continue to subsidise what is essentially a decaying building. The council won't spend a penny on it; they obviously want it closed.'

He knew! He knew she was the schoolmistress; she could feel it in her bones. He was playing with her, like a cat with a mouse. Losing her job was going to be payment for the way she had treated him today.

'Oh, but Candy is the teacher there,' her mother said quickly, 'and the children so love her.'

'You're the teacher?' He turned to face her now and as she met the full force of his cold blue stare her suspicions were confirmed. Yes, he had known. It was written in every line of his proud, arrogant face, and the small, menacing twist to his mouth would have convinced her if nothing else had. 'Dear, dear.' He raked back his hair, so dark a brown as to be almost black now the bleached ends had gone. 'Well, we'll have to confer about this, won't we?'

She glared back at him, too angry to consider what she said. 'I'm sure you'll do exactly what you want to regardless of anyone else's feelings, Mr Strythe.' His eyebrows rose mockingly as she gave him his full title. 'You did ten years ago, and a leopard doesn't change its spots.'

Her last words had wiped away the small smile that had played round his mouth in satirical contempt as he had listened to her passionate outburst and now, as her face turned white with the realisation of what she had said in front of everyone, he slowly moved his gaze from hers after one searing glance of utter scorn.

'This is excellent, Mrs Clarke. My compliments to the chef.' The smooth, controlled voice was like a slap in the face and she sank back in her seat feeling quite mortified, like a small child who had unwittingly made a serious social blunder.

She kept her eyes on her plate for the next few minutes, looking neither to left nor right while her hot anger cooled and she gained control, and when she heard Cameron deep in conversation with his host, a small, meek man normally dwarfed by his shrew of a wife, she raised them slowly and looked his way.

The years had added to his appeal, she admitted grudgingly—if you liked cold, unfeeling robots, that was! He had always been tall and lean, but now his shoulders were powerfully developed with the muscled strength of a prime athlete. His hair had been cut short, very short, which accentuated the chiselled, hard features and steel-blue eyes with their surprisingly thick lashes. Not exactly good-looking in the usual mode, she reflected musingly, but she could imagine the ladies just falling into those strong arms, wanting to change the indifference in those sharp eyes into something else.

There was something about him—a detachment, an aloofness that would draw some women like a powerful amulet. He stood out from the crowd. He always had.

She flushed scarlet suddenly as she became aware of his dark, raised eyebrows, his eyes tight on her face. He had caught her staring and she was furious with herself. Whatever would he think?

'I would like to discuss the school's finances further, Candice.' She noticed he gave her her full name, and he must have remembered how much she hated it! 'Could you call at the house after work tomorrow?'

'I suppose so,' she said bitterly, her expression portraying that she thought it was a fruitless exercise. 'It takes me some time to clear up, so I'll be there about five. OK?'

'Fine,' he returned easily. 'I'll have some tea waiting.'

'Please don't bother.' This polite conversation was ridiculous after what had gone before, she thought irritably. Everyone could feel the undercurrents swirling like a heavy black flood.

'It's no bother.' His eyes had narrowed and she sensed again that brooding ruthlessness that seemed at the very essence of him now. 'Mrs Baines is an excellent housekeeper, as I'm sure you know.' She couldn't bring herself to smile and merely nodded abruptly, her eyes cold. 'I'm sure Candice will bring you up to date with what we decide,' he said now to her father.

'She's her own boss, Cam,' her father said quietly. 'Has been for years.'

'I don't doubt it.' There was a cutting note in Cameron's voice that everyone seemed to miss apart from her, Candy thought balefully. He thought he was so powerful, so omnipotent. Well, she would show him! If he expected her to grovel to keep the school open he had another think coming. Nothing, nothing on this earth would persuade her to do that. If she had to get another job, so be it. Her qualifications were good enough to get her in anywhere.

The rest of the evening was fairly uneventful, although the discord between Candy and Cameron fairly reverberated around the room and everyone was glad when it was time to leave.

As the others milled into the hall, selecting their coats from the fashionable antique hall-stand, Cameron caught Candy's arm, forcing her to stand still. 'At five, then. I'm looking forward to it.' The arrogantly threatening note irritated her and she raised her huge brown eyes to his lowered face, her expression sardonic.

'Of such is life's little pleasures made.' The scorn in her voice was unmistakable.

'Exactly.' Now his voice was chilling. 'I've waited a long time to see you all again.'

'We didn't go anywhere,' she bit back furiously, and he allowed himself a small, cold smile.

'So you didn't. My, you've changed. Quite unrecognisable.' It wasn't meant as a compliment and she didn't pretend to treat it as such.

'You, unfortunately, are just the same.' She was annoyed to find her senses were registering the fact that he smelt delicious and a strange little quiver was causing her stomach muscles to clench in protest. He was so very...male. She couldn't think of anyone else who wore their masculinity so aggressively.

'I seem to remember we got on all right in the old days,' he said mockingly, and she felt an almost overwhelming impulse to smack that imperious face hard!

'I was a child then,' she answered shortly, 'and children are very trusting. Then they grow up.'

'I gather that little dig is meant for me?' The nerve of the man! After all that had happened, to stand there looking so irritatingly pleased with himself!

'Candy! Are you coming?' David's voice sounded faintly possessive, and she caught the contemplative look in Cameron's eyes as David walked in with her coat, helping her into it with an unnecessary air of ownership.

As they made their goodbyes she was vitally aware of the tall dark figure looking on just behind his hosts, and once in the car she maintained a cool silence until David pulled up outside their house. 'Go on in, you two; I just want a word with David.' There was something in her tone that caught her mother's attention.

'It's been a long day, dear; why don't you —— ?'

'Mum, please. I won't be a minute.' Her tone was polite but uncompromising and her mother bowed to the inevitable. Candy guessed her mother had sensed what she was about to say and wanted to talk her out of it. She had been hoping for some time that she and David would become more than friends, but had known better than to come straight out with her matchmaking.

Once they were alone she turned to David with eyes that were uncharacteristically hard. 'What have you got to say for yourself?'

'What about?' He couldn't hold her gaze. His eyes dropped to the dashboard and he fiddled with the radio, settling on a loud pop programme that grated round the car.

'You knew he would be there tonight, didn't you? Was he there when you left to fetch us?'

'No, of course not.' She knew he was lying; it was in every weak line of his face.

'Well, as far as I'm concerned you've let me down badly. I don't trust you.' She spoke in a quiet, reasonable tone, and for a moment the impact of her words didn't strike home, and then his face turned a dull red.

'Now look here, Candy —— '

'No, you look here.' She still was speaking quietly, but now there was a throbbing anger in her voice that made him shift uncomfortably in his seat. 'I happen to think that friendship is an important thing and I expect my friends to support me as I do them. You knew that man would be there tonight and you also knew all the history. I don't happen to consider myself or my family entertainment for one of your mother's sick schemes. What she did tonight was malicious and spiteful and you backed her all the way.'

'This is ridiculous...' His voice faded as she opened the car door jerkily.

'Goodbye, David.' She banged the car door with such ferocity that it bounced open again, but she entered the house without a backward glance.

What an evening! As she lay in bed, gazing up in the darkness to the pale glow of the ceiling, she could have almost laughed if it weren't all so tragic. She had lost her job and David in one fell swoop, although the latter she was well rid of, and it looked as though her little band of children, more like family than anything else, were going to be turned out of their school and forced to make the journey to Chitten. Her heart gave a little wrench as she pictured them one by one in her mind. Little Ann Cartwright was doing so well, in spite of her severe speech impediment, but she would just shrivel up in the anonymity of a big school, and Kevin... Now she couldn't stop the hot tears from seeping out of her eyes. He had lost his father recently in a farming accident and was still at the stage where he was clinging to her all day long. He would never cope with a change of schools.

How she hated Cameron Strythe! She sat up in bed suddenly and clenched her fists in helpless frustration. The man was a monster, a cold, unfeeling monster. Well, he couldn't just come back and wreck all their lives for the second time. She bit on her lip until she tasted blood. She would stop him. She didn't know how, but she would stop him, if it was the last thing she ever did. She wouldn't rest until he was crushed and broken...as Michelle had been on that night so long ago when he had left the house with his head held high and she had raced into the sitting-room to hear her sister moaning like an animal, crouched on her knees on the carpet.

She would wait until either fate or opportunity put a weapon in her hands and then she would use it, without pity and with no regard for his feelings.

He would find that the younger Baker sister wasn't such a push-over as her big sister. She would play him at his own game—and win!

CHAPTER TWO

IN THE cold light of day Candy woke up to the knowledge that Cameron Strythe was holding all the aces and she hated Monday mornings! The school was always freezing owing to being unoccupied all weekend, and the huge, unsightly radiators that were so inefficient always took all day to get the place warm.

After fixing a light breakfast of toast and coffee she sat curled up on the sitting-room window-seat watching the rain pour down outside. 'Come down to earth, girl,' she muttered to herself as she sipped the hot liquid slowly. 'You haven't got an earthly against him.' It would be the easiest thing in the world to close down the school; the council had been angling for it for years. It had only been Colonel Strythe's influence on the various committees he attended, plus the big, fat allowance he made the school each year, that

36

had kept it open this far, and obviously all that had come to an end.

'Oh, Jasper...' She allowed herself the brief indulgence of wallowing in self-pity for a few moments, her head buried in the warm, thick fur of the golden retriever, then squared her shoulders determinedly. Well, she might not be able to fight him with regard to the school, but she wouldn't leave a stone unturned to make his victory as empty as possible.

'Good morning, Miss Baker.' For the second time since his return Cameron forced her to give an exclamation of surprise as she swung round from the blackboard mid-morning to see him standing just inside the classroom door. 'I hope I'm not intruding?' His eyes dared her to speak her mind with the children watching and expressed malicious satisfaction when she forced herself to speak pleasantly.

'Not at all, Mr Strythe. What can I do for you?'

'I just thought I would pop in and see you at work,' he answered coolly. 'I trust you have no objection.'

'What a pity.' Her eyes darted black fire, but her mouth was smiling for the little on-lookers surveying them so interestedly. 'It's time for the children's playtime.' As she provided each child with a carton of milk and an apple, another of Colonel Strythe's blessings, she was aware of Cameron taking note of the crumbling plaster and creaking floorboards, but ignored him pointedly. 'It's stopped raining, children. All out into the playground. Mrs Harris has just arrived.'

When the last child had left the room and she had checked that they were all safely in the small playground with Karen Harris, one of the mother-helpers, she turned to Cameron with a frankly hostile expression on her face. 'Well?'

'You know, you really do have the most charming way with you,' he drawled slowly as he walked over to the empty picnic basket and flicked the lid with one finger. 'And who provides this little service each day? And don't tell me the council, because they gave free milk up years ago.'

'It was never given up at this school,' Candy answered coldly. 'Your father always saw to it that the required number of cartons of milk and apples were delivered each morning.'

'And who twisted his arm for that little act of generosity?' His voice was purposely insulting.

'I have no idea,' she returned acidly, 'considering I was merely a child myself at the time. Does it matter? Your father liked children, unlike some men.' She didn't even try to hide the meaning behind her barbed words.

'Meaning I don't?' There was an element of bewilderment in his face.

'Jamie is nearly ten years old now.' She had clearly lost him along the way; she could see it in the narrowing puzzlement of those piercing blue eyes. 'Jamie, Michelle's child.' His face hardened at the explanation and his mouth straightened into a thin, cruel line.

'So?' He was looking down at her in spite of her considerable height. He must be at least six feet four, she thought irrelevantly, and then returned to the attack, annoyed that her mind could wander at a moment like this.

'*So*?' She could feel the colour of her cheeks was matching the red of her hair but she didn't care. This man was incredible, absolutely incredible! 'Aren't you even interested in seeing him?'

'Any particular reason why I should be?' he said coldly, his face thundery.

She was saved the necessity of a reply by a timid knocking at the door that led into the playground. 'Please, miss...' Little Julie Roberts was standing on the threshold with one arm supportively round Kevin's thin, trembling shoulders. 'He wants you.'

'What's wrong, Kevin?' She went down on her heels in front of the small, woebegone figure, who lifted a grubby, tear-stained face up to her with a loud sniff.

'I want me mam.'

'You know she's coming for you later, after work, and Grandma is picking you up for lunch, isn't she?' He nodded dismally, a wealth of sadness in his large blue eyes. She rose up with him in her arms and carried him over to her chair, ignoring Cameron as though he didn't exist.

'It's your birthday soon, isn't it?' She had found in the last few weeks since his father had died that distraction was the best policy, combined with a close cuddle. He nodded again, looking up at her quickly.

'How old will you be?'

'You know, miss.' He wriggled delightedly at her asking.

'Oh, yes.' She pretended to consider a moment. 'Twenty-one, isn't it?'

'Six.'

'Six?' She clapped a hand over her mouth in mock horror. 'But you're enormous! You aren't kidding me, are you?' He shook his head, but she noticed that the tears had dried up and a small smile was playing round the milk-stained mouth.

'I bet you'll get lots of presents.' She knew for a fact that half the village had already bought the small lad a gift, stunned and horrified as they all were at the tragic accident.

'I can't have a party.' He turned his great eyes up to her again. 'Me mam hasn't got enough pennies this year.' He was clearly going to follow the train of thought that would lead him to why and his father's death, so she cut in quickly, her voice bright.

'Oh, we're having a party here for you,' she improvised rapidly. 'A big cake and streamers and everything.'

'And balloons?' His face had suddenly become alight and she smiled as she nodded vigorously.

'Of course, lots of balloons. Do you want to go and tell the other children now and then you can all start looking forward to it.'

'Me tell them?' This was clearly the icing on the cake and he slid off her lap and marched to the door, his thin shoulders squared with importance.

'What was all that about?' She had almost forgotten Cameron was there, but now he moved round to her side from where he had been standing leaning quietly against the wall. 'Do you have parties for all the children?'

She felt it was another criticism on needless expenditure and glared at him angrily, her face burning. 'Of course not, but Kevin has lost his father recently and there's only him and his mother. The grandparents help, but she's finding it hard and the pair of them aren't over the first shock yet.'

'Is that Mike Wilson's son?' His voice was harsh. She nodded slowly.

'I read the report on that yesterday. It happened on my father's property, didn't it? The man pulled down a load of stacked logs on himself when he was drunk.'

'He'd been drinking the night before, yes,' Candy answered tightly, 'but I understand the accident was just one of those things.'

'Hardly.' Cameron's voice was cold. 'The insurance company don't want to know. There was no negligence on my father's part, just sheer stupidity on Wilson's side. From the amount of alcohol still in his system I'm amazed he could have stood up. I'm afraid the family won't get a penny in damages.'

'They already know that,' she answered shortly, astounded by his lack of compassion. 'And don't worry, they have no intention of trying to get you to pay anything.' She almost spat the words at him. He was worse than ever she had imagined. She would never have believed a human being could be so devoid of even the most elementary tenderness. There had been no sympathy in his voice, just cold, harsh censure and biting condemnation.

'I'm aware of that,' he answered abruptly, his dark head tilted to one side as he considered her furious face. 'You're determined to cast me in the role of wicked black baron, aren't you? Do you always make such snap judgements? I wouldn't have thought in your line of profession that was very wise.' There it was again, that subtle criticism of her capabilities!

'It's no snap judgement where you are concerned,' she answered bitingly. 'I've had ten years to make up my mind about you.'

'And hating me for every one of them?' he asked mockingly.

'Dead right.' She turned and looked him full in the face. 'To me you are the lowest thing that ever walked this earth, Cameron Strythe; a fly-blown maggot is more appealing than you.'

'A doubtful comparison, but I think I get the message.' The man was so infuriatingly in control, she thought wildly, as he moved lazily towards the door from which he had entered. He turned on the threshold and held her with his icy blue gaze. 'Do I take it I am the heartless villain and your sister is the pure white innocent in this vivid imagination of yours?'

'She was pregnant with your child and you walked out on her,' Candy answered baldly. 'Those are the facts; you can't change them.'

'And if I denied that?'

'I wouldn't believe you.'

'I thought so.' The light from the window was turning her hair into glowing fire as she stood looking at him, her eyes great black pools of pain in her chalk-white face. He shook his head slowly, his face closed against her.

'Oh, what a tangled web we weave...'

'What?' Her voice was sharp and he shook his head again, his face clearing.

'Five tonight at the house, Candy.'

'You still want me to come?' She stared at him in surprise. She had thought after this little exchange there would be nothing left to say. She wouldn't have been surprised if he had come back and pinned a notice on the door stating the school was closed until further notice!

He nodded abruptly as he left, leaving her staring miserably at the empty doorway. What a mess! What a hopeless, impossible mess. She wondered how long it would be before he could close them down. There would be official channels to go through and such like, but with Colonel Strythe gone their only support had vanished, and the council would be quick to point that out. Six months, nine months, certainly no more. The council had been waiting for an opportunity like this for years.

The first faint fingers of dusk were touching the blue-grey sky as she made her way towards the farm later that day. Normally she would have enjoyed the walk to the Strythe house, taking pleasure in the small humpbacked bridge below which the crystal-clear waters of the gurgling stream were forded by stepping-stones, and the huge, sweeping drive lined with evergreen yews, oaks and beech trees, but today the beauty around her was wasted. Her whole being was concentrated on the confrontation ahead and she was dreading it. She wished Charles Strythe hadn't died; she wished Cameron hadn't come back; she wished so many things...

'Hello, Miss Candy.' Mrs Baines ushered her into the wide wood-panelled hall with a beaming smile. 'It's lovely to see you again, makes it seem more like old times.' The round red-cheeked face took on a sober expression that didn't sit well on the plump little woman. Mrs Baines had been with Colonel Strythe as long as she could remember, Candy mused; she must be missing him dreadfully. 'Come to see Mr Cameron, I understand? You go into the drawing-room and I'll tell him you're here.'

Candy made her way to the drawing-room, looking round this room she had always loved as she entered. The Strythe house was built more in the style of a country mansion than of the average farmhouse seen scattered through the county. The rooms were large and high, with beautifully sculptured ceilings and vast window-seats, thick, deep carpets and long velvet curtains.

The grounds around the house were lovingly cared for and the stables situated some distance away were always in pristine condition, housing some fine mounts. According to her father, the Strythe family had diversified into many other areas besides farming, creating enormous wealth, although the family home with its acres of prime Devonshire cattle and sheep had always been Colonel Strythe's first love.

She glanced at his portrait now as she stood before the roaring log fire waiting for Cameron's arrival, noting the light blue eyes, the firm mouth and that small dimple in his chin that Cameron had inherited too. She missed him. She really did. The beautiful room, with its rich deep red curtains and upholstery and fine antique furniture, seemed empty without his benign presence.

'I'm sorry to have kept you waiting.' She hadn't noticed Cameron come in, lost as she was in the past, and started violently for the third time since his homecoming. 'Do you suffer with your nerves?' From anyone else the question, asked as it was in quiet, concerned tones, might have been genuine, but as she looked into his eyes she saw dark devilment gleaming out at her.

'No, I do not,' she returned sharply, flushing hotly.

'Do I make you nervous, then?' He had moved closer to her as he spoke and for the second time she became aware of that tantalising smell that was a part of him. It stirred something deep inside her that she would prefer not to be stirred.

'No.' As she spoke the denial she realised it was a lie. He did make her nervous, horribly nervous, and that in turn made her angry.

'Good,' he said lazily. He had changed since that morning and, looking at him in casual trousers and a heavy Aran sweater, she became aware that he really was quite devastatingly attractive. She caught her wandering thoughts savagely. She hadn't really just thought that...had she?

'You wanted to see me?' She kept her voice cool and businesslike and walked with studied calm from the comforting warmth of the fire to the big easy-chair near by, perching on the end of it and crossing her hands on her lap.

'Now I can almost believe you are a school-teacher when you look like that,' he said mockingly as he took in her stiff stance. 'Although with that hair and those eyes it's almost impossible to comprehend.'

'What do you mean?' she asked furiously. 'Schoolteachers are people; we come in all shapes and sizes.'

'There aren't many with a shape like yours,' he countered quickly. 'You can't tell me you were short of male admirers when you were at university. I've been there; I know what a female like you about the place would do to the male population.' There was some element in his voice she couldn't place and she stared at him uncertainly for a moment.

'I've had boyfriends, yes,' she said slowly, disliking the way the conversation was going. 'No more and no less than any other girl, I suppose.'

'Anyone special?' His voice was casual.

'Look, I really don't think that's any of your business,' she said sharply. 'I'm here to discuss the school's future—or lack of it,' she added bitterly. 'Shall we get on with it?'

'Impatient little puss, aren't you?' he said mockingly, smiling slightly as she glared back at him. 'But I suppose you were destined to be prickly and bad-tempered with hair the colour of fire.'

'I am not prickly or bad-tempered—usually,' she added pointedly, 'and please cut the chit-chat. You won't charm me, Mr Strythe, so don't try.'

'I wouldn't dream of it,' he said cryptically.

It was some time later when Mrs Baines brought in the tea-trolley and by then Candy had to admit that putting money into the school in a business sense was like pouring it down the drain. She couldn't justify Cameron's continuing his father's patronage in any financial argument, but then Colonel Strythe hadn't looked on it as an investment in any other sense but a human one. He had known how much the villagers wanted their children taught locally, he had seen how happy their offspring were in familiar surroundings, and once he had satisfied himself that the academic standard was good enough he had been more than prepared to be magnanimous. He could afford it, he had once told Candy, and the amount he spared the school and village was lost in the Strythe finances. Obviously his son thought differently!

She glared at him now as he gravely thanked Mrs Baines and took the heavy trolley from her, opening the door for her to leave. He could be so sickeningly pleasant when he pleased, but he didn't fool her for a minute. She had seen what loving him had done to her sister, and Colonel Strythe had never been the same again once his son had left. This man left devastation and havoc wherever he went. She wondered how many broken hearts were scattered across Australia.

'I won't say, "a penny for your thoughts", because frankly I think I would be better not knowing,' the deep, husky voice said cynically. She focused her eyes sharply, aware she had been gazing at him with her thoughts far away. 'Help yourself to sandwiches and cake and please try to force yourself to eat, whatever you think of the present company. Mrs Baines will be most upset if most of this doesn't disappear.'

Candy had always been blessed with a particularly robust appetite that rarely faltered whatever the circumstances, and the selection of wafer-thin sandwiches, temptingly filled rolls, tiny individual pork pies and mouthwatering homemade cakes was too good to resist. Cameron had pulled two easy-chairs closer to the fire before bringing the trolley to her side, switching on the television as he sat down. It was too cosy, too companionable, but she was hungry, and by concentrating on the flickering screen she found she had demolished a good proportion of the food by the time she was full. She looked up to find a pair of amused steel-blue eyes fixed on her face.

'Good grief, girl, do you always eat like that?' His gaze roved down her slender figure in wonder.

'You did say to eat...whatever I think of the present company.' The last was added with wry defiance and she swung back her heavy fold of rich silky hair from her shoulders. 'I had better be going now. You've made your point about the school; I really don't think —— '

'I haven't made any point as far as I'm aware and we most certainly have not finished this discussion,' he said curtly as he rang the bell by the side of the fireplace. When Mrs Baines had cleared the remains of the meal, exclaiming in pleasure at the appreciation of her cooking, he closed the door behind her and moved back to his chair, turning off the television as he did so.

'There is another point I want to discuss with you, Candy, so forget the school problem for a moment.' She resented hearing her nickname on his lips almost as much as she had done when he had called her Candice. The poor man can't win, she thought wryly, except that no one in their right mind would ever describe Cameron Strythe as a poor man.

'Your father is the same age as mine, I understand?' She stared at him blankly. What on earth had her father's age to do with anything?

'I've no idea. I suppose they must be close in age; they grew up together, after all.'

'Well, at sixty I think your father deserves some years without having the responsibility of what is a very taxing job on his shoulders. If Dad had taken it easier he might still be here now.'

She stared at him as the meaning of his words filtered through to her brain. 'You aren't going to sack him? You can't!' She rose abruptly to her feet, her eyes tragic.

'Don't be so ridiculous, woman.' His voice cut through her like a razor. 'I'm talking about retirement.'

'Retirement?' she mumbled. 'But he doesn't want to retire. The cottage and every-thing—where would they live?' This last tack had taken her by surprise and for a moment she couldn't get her mind to function properly, and then, as hot, blinding rage took over, she took a step towards him, drawing him to his feet by her fury.

'You swine; you total, absolute swine!' She was too enraged to see how white his face had gone and how those cold eyes had become positively arctic. 'You come back here after all this time and what do you do?' She was almost incoherent in her anger. 'First you are going to close down the school and I don't know what Kevin will do...' She gave a gasping sob as she took breath. 'And then Dad: you're going to take out your spite on Dad as well. And what have we done to you? It was you who messed up our lives; you've had a rare old time...making your fortune in Australia, and now everything is yours —— '

'Stop it.' He had reached her side in one stride and took her arms in his hands, shaking her slightly as her voice rose to the edge of hysteria. 'Control yourself.'

'Control myself?' Her voice was a shriek, but she couldn't have stopped the avalanche if she had wanted to and she didn't want to. She wanted to scream and yell at him, wanted to claw his face with her hands. She hated him, oh, she did, so much.

As his hand came across her face in a sharp slap the surprise of it cut off her voice as though with a knife and then the next minute he had pulled her into his arms, holding her shaking figure close as he talked in quiet, reasonable tones. 'I'm sorry, Candy, but I had to do that; you were going to make yourself ill.' She wanted to struggle, wanted to fight him, but suddenly the adrenalin had all gone and it was only his hands on her body keeping her upright.

'You haven't given me a chance to explain, to make you understand.' He was speaking into the soft silk of her hair, her head pressed into the front of his chest, and now he lifted her face with one hand, gazing down into the tear-drenched huge eyes. 'How can anyone so beautiful be so obstinate?' There was a note in his voice she didn't dare dwell on, but it made her want to cry even more. 'What is it with you, carrot-tops?'

As his mouth came down on hers she knew she ought to resist. This was Cameron, who had used her sister so badly and now was ripping her safe little world apart, but with a sense of horror she realised she had been waiting for this since the first time she had seen him again. He was so different to any other man she had ever met, so...

As the kiss deepened his probing lips opened hers with effortless ease, speaking of his practised seduction, but although she recognised his expertise she was powerless to stop him. It was a kiss, only a kiss, and yet he had her whole body trembling and aching as though they had been making love for hours. She had always laughed at those books that spoke of the heroine becoming helpless under the hero's passion, but she was experiencing it now!

'So sweet, so very, very sweet...' His breath was hot and clean as his mouth moved to her throat, kissing the pulse beating so frantically until she thought she would faint with the thrill of it. He had her pressed close into his body, moulding her shape to his, and as she became aware of his arousal she knew a moment's bitter-sweet satisfaction that he wanted her; he wanted her and he couldn't hide the fact.

As his tongue ravaged the secret places of her mouth she knew a sensual pleasure she had never experienced before, hardly conscious that he was moving down her throat and still down to the soft swell of her breasts, moving aside her blouse with practised ease. His hands and mouth were both tender and forceful and she was mesmerised by it all, by this delicious intoxication that had taken over her whole body.

Somewhere, dimly, she heard a telephone ringing, but that was in another world. Her world was here in this room, with a growing, whirling crescendo of feeling, and the soft, crackling glow of the fire red against her closed eyelids.

The tap on the door and Mrs Baines's voice acted like a draught of cold water. She jerked violently out of Cameron's arms, glancing wildly at the closed door, and then became fully aware of the state of her undress as she stood swaying and dazed in the middle of the room.

'Just a moment, Mrs Baines.' Cameron's voice was unforgivably cool, and she knew a second's intense, burning humiliation as he waited for her to fasten the tiny silver buttons of her blouse and straighten her tumbled hair before moving across the room. She heard Mrs Baines's voice, but couldn't distinguish what she said through the drumming in her ears. What had she done? *What had she done*? To fall into his arms like that! After everything she had said, after everything he had done!

She glanced frantically at the closed door and heard Cameron's voice, low and controlled, talking to someone in the hall. He must be on the telephone. How was she going to face him again? How was she going to endure the cool, sardonic mockery that those ice-blue eyes managed so well?

She looked towards the window hidden behind thick velvet full-length curtains. She knew the dining-room windows led on to the bowling-green-smooth lawns at the back of the house. How often she had played there as a young child while the rest of the two families socialised inside, running in and out with garlands of daisies and handfuls of buttercups picked from the small copse beyond the lawns, and later she had often sat in the shade of the big oak bordering the lawns with Uncle Charles while Mrs Baines served them tea.

She didn't think about her actions; she just knew she had to escape before Cameron returned. It was easy to slip out through the full-length windows, shutting them carefully behind her, and then she ran like a young deer across the lawns until she reached the drive, only feeling safe once she was on the road that skirted the village. She was halfway home, keeping to the shadows, before she realised she had left her bag with its mass of homework corrections sitting by the side of her chair in the dining-room. 'Damn, damn, damn...' She ground her teeth angrily. Well, she couldn't go back now. There was no way she was facing him again tonight. She would rather walk through fire backwards.

There was only Jasper to greet her when she reached home, for which she was supremely thankful. After fixing herself a cup of coffee, she carried it with her into her bedroom, drinking it down in hot, reviving gulps as she ran a warm, scented bath. She needed to soak, soak away the seductive memory of his hands and mouth on her flesh, the sense of burning betrayal of Michelle she was feeling that had her gazing wide-eyed at her reflection in the mirror as though staring at a stranger.

'How could you, Candy? How could you do that?' The white-faced girl looking back at her could give her no answer.

As she stepped into the bath she heard the phone ring stridently downstairs and her stomach jumped into her mouth. She paused, with one leg in the water, relaxing only when it stopped and all was quiet again. Within minutes she heard Jasper barking delightedly and her father's voice, and then seconds later, as she was washing her hair, digging her fingers into her scalp until it hurt, the phone rang again.

'Candy?' Her mother's voice sounded outside the bathroom door. 'Cam's on the phone. Can you take it?'

'No, sorry.' Her voice sounded amazingly normal. 'I've just got in the bath.'

'Oh, right.' Her mother's voice sounded faintly perplexed but she heard footsteps padding downstairs and she was left in peace again.

As she lay in the thick, scented water, the bubbles covering her arms and legs, hot resentment took the place of the crushing humiliation that had had her in its grip. He had tried that little seduction scene on purpose; he must think she was crazy! How low could a man get? She sat up straight in her anger, the water running in diamond rivulets down her back. He was going to close the school and sack her father, however he wanted to dress it up. That was what it amounted to, and he thought that bit of cheap lovemaking could ease the blow. Maybe he thought that having got one sister twisted round his little finger so many years ago he would have no trouble with the other one. She ground her teeth in helpless frustration. And she hadn't exactly led him to believe differently, had she? She groaned and slid under the water for a few seconds, holding her breath as the hot water washed across her face.

What else was he going to do now he was back and so powerful? He had virtually written poor Kevin's mother off without a penny; he obviously didn't care about the village, the people, anything. There was no reason why he should, but surely a little compassion wouldn't hurt too much? As she came up for air she realised her mind was going round in circles and climbed wearily out of the bath.

She would fight him—more than ever now she would fight him—but one thing she had learnt tonight. He fought dirty and if she wanted to win she had to fight dirtier still. She squared her shoulders under the thick, fleecy towelling-robe as her eyes glinted with the light of battle. 'So be it, Cameron Strythe,' she muttered into the steamy, damp room. 'No holds barred, just the way you want it.'

CHAPTER THREE

'AND where the hell did you get to last night?'
Candy had expected mockery or cool indifference, but nothing had prepared her for the
furious, rapier-sharp voice that speared her as
she sat at her desk at lunchtime with the sound
of the children's laughter echoing in from the
playground.

'I beg your pardon?' She rounded indig-
nantly to find Cameron standing in the
doorway like before, but this time his face was
dark with anger and his eyes were as cold as
ice.

'You will beg; before I'm finished with you
I can assure you you will beg!' His voice was
a low snarl and if she hadn't been seated she
was sure her legs would have given way at the
savagery in his face as he flung her bag on the
floor.

'I searched the grounds for you and then
the village. I didn't know where you'd gone,
you little idiot!'

'Home, of course.' She glared at him angrily. 'You phoned, didn't you? You know that.'

'You've got a nerve. You Baker sisters take some beating for sheer, cold-blooded nerve.' She realised with a start of surprise that his voice was fairly shaking with anger and something else she couldn't fathom.

'What?' He'd lost her here.

'Nothing.' He waved away her question with a weary gesture of contempt. 'I don't believe this; I don't believe I'm actually bothering to talk to you instead of taking you over my knee and giving you the thrashing of your life.'

'You just try it!' She reared up like a small tigress and his eyes narrowed with hated amusement.

'Don't tempt me, just don't tempt me.'

She had been wondering all morning how she would face him again after the travesty of the night before, but at least that hurdle was over, she reflected wryly as she watched him pace the room. It was comforting somehow that he wasn't his normal cool, sardonic self, although she couldn't have explained why. His anger was preferable to that mocking coldness that chilled her blood.

'If you ever, ever do anything like that again I won't be responsible for my actions.' He had come to stand in front of her desk and she stared at him from behind its comforting bulk.

'I don't think that sort of situation will ever arise again, so you needn't worry yourself on that score,' she said tightly. 'If you will go around leaping on women you should expect——'

'Leaping on you?' He stared at her astounded for a moment and then she was furious to see him throw back his head and bellow a peal of laughter that echoed round the high ceiling. 'Is that what you've decided happened in that busy little brain of yours?' He had stopped laughing now, but there was a cruel twist to his mouth. 'Listen, sweetheart, I was there; I know what happened and so do you.' His voice was punishingly hard. 'I've no intention of labouring the point, but you enjoyed it as much as I did—and I did.' He eyed her up and down in insulting slowness. 'Yes, I sure did. You pack quite a punch after that touch-me-not act.'

She felt the hot colour start in her toes and work upwards. She'd asked for this, but how he was enjoying it! She maintained an icy silence, staring him straight in the eye, and he shook his head slowly as he turned away and walked to the door.

'I haven't worked all this out yet, but I will,' he said coolly. 'And if it's as I think then some people have got a hell of a lot of explaining to do.'

'What?' She stared after him, baffled. 'I don't know what you're talking about.'

'And in the meantime,' he continued as though she hadn't spoken, 'you'll keep a civil tongue in your head, young lady.'

'You can't tell me what to do,' she fired back quickly, her brown eyes glowing with rage.

'No?' He paused in the doorway with a cynical smile touching his lips. 'Think again. You want the school to stay open and you want your father to keep his job?'

'You . . .' Words failed her, but the message in her eyes was piercingly eloquent.

'Exactly. I'm the lowest thing that ever drew breath, so just remember that when you feel like defying me.' She had thought she couldn't hate him any more, but she was finding new boundaries to her emotions every day.

'I'm having a small dinner party at the end of the week to break the ice with old friends and you'll be there.' He looked at her unsmilingly. 'You'll be sweet and you'll be charming and absolutely delighted to have me home. Understand?'

'That's blackmail.' Her voice was a disgusted whisper.

'Not quite the word I would have chosen, but I see you get my drift,' he said caustically. 'You have done nothing but provoke and insult me since I got back and one thing you need to learn fairly rapidly is that I won't tolerate it. This can be learnt relatively painlessly or the hard way, and frankly I don't care which way you choose, but, Candy...' he eyed her coldly ' ...you *will* learn it.'

'You can't make me——'

'Careful, Candy; think before you speak,' he said cynically. 'You have a habit of rushing in where angels fear to tread and although you're a very independent and determined young woman I've discovered your Achilles' heel. You care, really care about this village and its inhabitants and you love your family.'

'And you're going to use that against me?' She stared at him, white-faced and stony-eyed.

'If that's the way you want to put it, yes.' His eyes were hard and penetrating without a trace of mercy in their blue depths. 'I've had quite enough of your rudeness over the last two days and I don't intend it to continue. Right?'

She stood up slowly, her burning cheeks in stark contrast to the paleness of before. 'Why can't you just leave us all alone? Why did you have to come back anyway? We don't need you here; you're an outsider now.'

If it had been anyone else she would have thought it was pain that seared the chiselled features as he stared back at her so grimly, but Cameron Strythe feeling pain...never!

'Be that as it may, I stand by what I say,' he said coldly. 'I've got more than enough to do over the next few weeks without concerning myself with trivialities.'

Trivialities! She glared at him furiously as she ground her teeth to keep the flood of hot words from tumbling out. How dared he refer to them all as trivialities? She swallowed audibly.

'That's it; you're learning.' There was something in the drawling voice that didn't ring true and for a brief moment she felt he was enjoying this as little as she was, but one glance at the set, hard face convinced her differently. How could someone change so much in the passage of a few years? The old Cameron, bad as he was, would have been incapable of such cold-blooded cruelty. But then she hadn't really known *him* in those golden years of childhood. Her romantic ideal of a dark, shining knight in white armour had been brutally ground into the dust that summer evening so long ago and she realised with a small dart of surprise that she still bore the scars of that night deep in the secret recesses of her heart. He had left them all without a backward glance, left her...

She forced her mind away from the path it was taking, suddenly horrified by her thoughts. 'I think you are totally despicable.'

'I know.' There was no emotion in his voice.

She got through the rest of the day working on automatic, and by evening a dull, persistent headache had settled behind her eyes and all she wanted was a bath and bed. Dark clouds were scudding across the sky as she walked home and the wind was ferocious, whipping the bare, groaning branches of the trees with its icy fingers as it roared by, almost carrying her along in its path. She normally loved walking back through the village, but found herself regretting she hadn't driven to work that morning in her cheerful little red Mini. She felt cold and irritable and tired, and the fifteen-minute walk felt like an hour's by the time she reached home.

As she turned into the driveway she was surprised to see a dark red sports car sitting patiently outside the double garage. A Lamborghini, no less. Her gaze roved over the long, sleek lines as her mind considered whom they knew who could possibly afford such a flamboyant showpiece of a car. No one, unless . . .

It was with a feeling of resigned doom that she entered the house, expecting the low, deep,

distinct voice that met her ears, but still un-
prepared for its effect as her stomach gave a
small, protesting jerk.

'Hi.' Her polite smile and nod included
both Cameron and her mother in its sweeping
neutrality, but as she took in the teacups and
empty plates she had to force her face to
remain bland and expressionless.

'We've been waiting for you,' her mother
said cheerfully, her eyes bright and her cheeks
flushed. 'I told Cam you're always ready for
a cup of tea when you get home.'

'Yes...' She couldn't keep the smile in place
any longer. How dared he ingratiate himself
into her home like this when all the time he
planned to stab her father in the back? 'Sorry,
but I've got a wicked headache. Could I take
mine upstairs with a couple of aspirin?'

'Oh.' Her mother looked extremely flus-
tered as Candy divested herself of her coat
and scarf and poured them all tea, picking up
her cup immediately and making for the door.
'Did you see Cam's car?' she asked brightly
as Candy reached the doorway. 'Isn't it a
beauty?'

'I could hardly miss it,' Candy answered drily as she turned to meet Cameron's tight, watchful gaze, which held more than a touch of steel in its depths. 'And it's very in keeping with what I would have expected you to drive,' she added directly.

'Is that so?' He was looking dangerously attractive, the bronzed darkness of his skin accentuated by the light cream trousers and sweater he was wearing, making his hair black in contrast. 'How so?'

It was a challenge, and one Candy would have loved to accept, but she contented herself with a scornful smile and a casual wave of her hand. 'Oh, you know, long, sleek, powerful...' Ostentatious, pretentious, conspicuous... The unsaid words hung in the air and she knew he had read her mind. It was there in the musing narrowing of his eyes and the hard set of his jaw.

'Your father would have loved a car like that once, but it's a young man's machine,' her mother prattled on happily, oblivious to the tension.

'Or a young woman's,' Cameron said slowly, his eyes still on Candy's face. 'Have you ever driven a sports car?'

She shook her head reluctantly, wishing she could have surprised him.

'Would you like to?' She stared at him, unsure if he was serious, but the cold face was closed and still.

'I suppose so.' She shrugged lightly. 'I like speed.'

'I'll call round for you tomorrow night—when your headache's better,' he added sardonically. 'A friend of mine owns a race-track a few miles away; you can have a try there. If you like speed I don't want you tempted on the narrow country lanes round here.'

'I'm not a complete idiot,' she said sharply, 'and it's all right; I wouldn't be insured and things...' She waved vaguely.

'I'll see to all that.' He fixed her with his piercing blue eyes. 'Not frightened, are you?'

'No.' She responded immediately and saw a smile flicker for a moment at the edge of the firm mouth.

'Five o'clock, then.'

She nodded silently, aware that her mother was less than ecstatic about the turn the conversation had taken. As she left the room she heard his low, husky voice speak reassuringly, and guessed he was pouring oil on troubled waters. What was he doing here? She sat on the edge of her bed, sipping the hot tea, and tried to ascertain his motives. He didn't need their approval for any changes he planned to make and she was sure he was the last person on earth to care about what people thought, so why this apparent cultivating of her parents' friendship and, more importantly still, why were her parents allowing it?

She frowned as the ache behind her eyes worsened. He was up to something—she could feel it—and, whatever it was, it wouldn't bode well for her. She didn't trust him an inch and she was amazed and desperately disappointed that her parents seemed willing to let bygones be bygones. Couldn't they see that he was worse, if anything, than before?

She was still in this uneasy state of mind when Cameron rang the doorbell promptly at five the next evening. 'All ready?' He grinned down at her on the doorstep, his dark leather jacket and bulky jumper making him even more intimidating.

Once in the car he turned to her before starting the engine. 'I was expecting a phone call all day to say you had changed your mind,' he said easily, 'but then as I was driving here I realised you'd rather die than have me suspect you were nervous. Am I right?'

'Not at all,' she lied firmly, her eyes hooded. 'Your opinion of me is the last thing I would worry about.'

'Maybe.' He was smiling as the powerful engine purred into life and unconsciously she chewed at her bottom lip as the car prowled out of the drive. She didn't like his easy reading of her mind and she liked the tense excitement she was feeling even less. It wasn't so much the proposed drive on the race-track that was causing her heart to pound and making her palms wet as the big body sitting in relaxed ease next to her. Her eyes slid to his muscled thighs and long legs and her stomach fluttered nervously. Physical attraction. It was just one of those things. It could happen any time and any place and it didn't mean anything. It was almost inevitable in the present circumstances, she told herself reasonably, with Cameron returning so unexpectedly with his air of mystery and coldness and his sensual good looks. He was probably perfectly aware where his appeal lay; he had probably even contrived it over the years. Well, this was one woman who could and would resist him; the other night was definitely a one-off. She was on her guard now.

'Could you stop frowning quite so determinedly?' There was more than a touch of amusement in the deep voice. 'I'm not going to make you do anything you don't want to.' Coming from him, that was the joke of the year, Candy thought furiously, her raised eyebrows speaking for themselves. 'Not on the race-track, anyway,' he amended with an infuriating grin.

'I still don't know why I'm here.' She spoke her thoughts out loud and he glanced at her fleetingly, his blue eyes glinting oddly.

'Because you can't resist a challenge, carrot-tops; you never could.'

'Don't call me that!' She knew her voice had been more in the tone of a bark, but hearing that old nickname now in view of the present circumstances was too much.

'Why not? You didn't used to object,' he murmured quietly.

'That was a different time in a different world,' she said bitterly, 'and you know it.'

'Maybe,' he admitted slowly. 'And this David? How much of a "friend" is he?'

The change in tack completely threw her and she stared at him for a moment in complete amazement before shutting her mouth with a little snap. 'My relationship with David is ——'

'Nothing to do with me?' He finished her sentence for her, his tone wry. 'Perhaps not, but I wouldn't like to see you make the biggest mistake of your life without saying anything.' He shifted position slightly and she tensed instinctively. Help, she breathed silently. If his motive in getting this automobile had been to add to his sexual charisma she had news for him—it had worked! The sleek, powerful car was like a projection of his own personality, and the two combined were dynamite. 'The man is a rat; can't you see that?'

She totally agreed with his analysis, but there was no way she was going to give him the satisfaction of telling him so. She shrugged nonchalantly, flicking back her heavy fold of hair as she spoke. 'I think I'm old enough to make up my own mind about what friends I choose, don't you?'

'I think you're old enough for a lot of things, sweetheart; that's what worries me.' It was said with humour, but she glared at the hard profile balefully.

'You aren't that much older than me, Cameron Strythe, so don't talk like my grandfather.'

'Your grandfather?' She was disconcerted to find his brilliant blue eyes fixed on her for a second and then he swung the car off the road on to the grass verge and cut the engine with a savage jerk. 'Let's get one thing straight, Candy,' he said slowly, all trace of amusement or mockery gone from his face. 'My feelings for you aren't in the least paternal, and I'm sorry to say ''brotherly'' doesn't fit the bill either. The little kitten I left

behind me ten years ago is a fully grown cat
and those claws are sharp. I know; I've felt
them.' His eyes dropped to her mouth for a
moment and then returned to meet her gaze.
'You are a very beautiful woman and I appreciate you as such. Does that satisfy you?'

'Oh, you . . .' He was twisting this all round
as though she had been fishing for compliments, and she hadn't.

'Added to which you have a good mind and
an exceptionally good body. The only thing
that mars perfection is this.' He tapped her
head gently. 'I don't think I've ever met such
a forceful young woman and, believe me, I've
met plenty.'

'I don't doubt it,' she said bitingly,
although something in her shrivelled at the
thought of the women he had had.

'Added to which,' he continued as though
she hadn't spoken, 'you have a very definite
vendetta against me, which I do not find attractive, considering there is no cause.'

'No cause?' She repeated his words in blank
amazement at his audacity, and he nodded
slowly as he lifted her chin with one finger.

'Absolutely no cause, as one day you will realise.'

'Never.' There was such a wealth of bitterness in her face that he drew back slightly, his head at a slight angle. 'I'll never forgive you for what you did to Michelle, Cameron, and since you've been home you've been . . . awful.' There wasn't a word to describe it all. 'And your father missed you so much for years.'

'Now I *know* you're fantasising.' This time the savage derision was on *his* face and he turned from her, starting the engine again, his eyes chips of blue glass. 'Cut out the hearts and flowers, Candy. If you're trying to make me feel guilty you are on the wrong track.' He swung the car sharply into the road after checking his mirrors. 'I know exactly where I stood with my father and I don't regret a thing.'

'I don't understand.' She stared at him, sick at his callousness. 'You left in the first place because you didn't have the courage to stay and face up to your responsibilities, and then you stayed away because you were having too good a time to come home. You broke his heart.'

He swore, softly and vehemently, and Candy's heart rose in her mouth as the car was swung again off the road. Before she had time to register what was happening he had cut the engine and pulled her roughly against him, his mouth hard against hers and his hands brutal on her arms. The kiss was ruthless and menacing and completely without a shred of tenderness, and when finally he threw her from him she sank into the corner of her seat, her eyes dazed and hurt and her mouth bruised. 'Does that satisfy you?' he asked bitterly. 'Does that come into line with how you think of me?' She couldn't answer, shocked to the core at his harsh mastery over her natural feminine weakness. He had used brute strength and she hated him for it, hated him!

'You don't know the first thing about life, do you?' he said furiously, his voice cutting through her like a knife. 'It's like listening to a child prattling about a fairy story they've read. When I was born I cost my father the one thing he had ever loved: his wife. He never forgave me for it.' The words hung in the air, stark and uncompromising, and his eyes raked her white face grimly. 'I had a nanny until the age of seven, who had strict instructions to keep me out of my father's way, and then I was packed off to boarding-school and allowed home, on occasion, at holiday time. For every achievement I attained, more was expected. I lived my life trying to justify my existence for years, until I realised I didn't have to. I didn't owe my father a thing, not a thing.' There was dark anger in his face and something else, something that tore at Candy's heart in spite of all he had done. It was a raw, hurt kind of misery that she had never imagined seeing on another human being's face.

'For what it's worth, I didn't leave here like a whipped dog.' The strange look had gone, replaced by fierce pride. 'I've done a few things in my life that I'm not too proud of, but leaving your sister was not one of them.'

Every vestige of pity fled her face as the shock of his words took hold. 'And Jamie?' she asked through numb lips.

'Forget it, Candy. Emotional blackmail is lost on me,' he said slowly and deliberately. 'Michelle has been dead to me from the night I left and if you hadn't been such a child you might have understood why.'

'I understood all right,' she said acidly. 'It wasn't exactly something that could be hidden, was it?'

He shook his head quietly, his face grim. 'You'll believe exactly what you want to believe, won't you?' he said softly. 'No grey, just black and white, good and bad. I don't know if I envy you that stubbornness or pity you for it. I know one thing: it's going to make you suffer one day.'

'It's people who make other people suffer,' she said bitterly, and he nodded slowly, his eyes bleak.

'How right you are.' They sat in silence for some minutes and she felt the raw emotion that had vibrated round the car had affected him more than he would care to admit, although his face retained its cold remoteness and his big body was relaxed. There was something here she didn't understand, a niggling doubt that was increasing each time she met him, but as yet it hadn't solidified into conscious thought. She just knew he had the power to turn her upside-down, mentally, physically, every which way, and she bitterly resented it.

As they drove off again she risked a quick glance at his set face from under her eye-lashes. He didn't expect her still to drive this thing, did he? Her nerves were in ribbons, but within ten minutes they turned into a long, narrow lane that led down to a huge, disused airfield which she saw had been converted into a rather disreputable race-track.

'Kirk is into stock-car racing,' Cameron said shortly as he drew on to the massive en-closure, raising a hand to someone in the dis-tance, who waved back. 'Are you ready?'

She passed a tongue over her dry lips and forced a brightness she was far from feeling into her voice. 'Yes, great.' Not for all the world would she let him know that this last confrontation with its searing revelations and brutality had caused a trembling deep inside that was making her feel physically ill. She would drive this great beast of a machine and drive it well!

As he got out of the car and walked round to the passenger side she slid over into his seat, which was still warm from his body heat. What was she doing; what *was* she doing?

'I'll just run through the basics with you and then it's over to you,' Cameron said quietly as he settled himself beside her. 'Don't try to get too familiar with her on the first day; just take it nice and steady and you'll find you'll enjoy yourself.' She looked at him sharply, but his eyes were on the controls as he began to talk. He had clearly sensed her nervousness and was trying to reassure her, and strangely, for once, his actions didn't grate on her.

An hour later and she was feeling immensely pleased with herself, having to bite back the grin that was threatening to spread across her face every few seconds. She had managed the powerful car well and thoroughly enjoyed herself in the process, much to her surprise. Cameron had been less than effusive about her capabilities, but she felt he had approved of her handling of the car, and now, as they drove home with Candy back in the passenger-seat again, she couldn't resist a sly little glance in his direction. 'I quite enjoyed that,' she said airily, and as he spared her a quick glance she saw his eyes crinkle slightly at the corners.

'Fishing for compliments, carrot-tops?' he said mockingly.

'No,' she said stoutly and then flushed as his mouth curled into a teasing grin. 'Well, perhaps yes. It wouldn't hurt you to say I did OK,' she added aggressively.

'You did more than OK; I was quite impressed,' he said quietly, 'but it was only what I expected.'

'Was it?' She felt the glow of satisfaction spread and then checked herself quickly. Clever, very clever, Cameron, she thought uneasily. Not the usual charm technique, but then that hadn't worked too well, had it? She wondered how many women he had allowed to drive his car, how many he had wooed...

'None.'

'What?' She eyed him cautiously, a pink flush staining her cheeks. She hadn't spoken out loud; she knew she hadn't!

'You were wondering how many females have driven this car before.' It was a cool statement and she longed to deny it, but the lie hesitated on her tongue.

She contented herself with a cold shrug instead, feigning sarcasm. 'You go in for mind-reading too?'

'I go in for all sorts of things, Candy; I thought you knew that.' There was a touch of bitterness in his voice and she eyed him again from under her thick lashes. He changed moods quicker than anyone she had ever met.

'You should have turned off there.' She went to touch his arm as they passed the crossroads leading into the village, but waved vaguely at the air instead.

'Hungry?' It seemed an answer as far as he was concerned and she stared at him uncertainly. 'Are you hungry?' he said again, a brusque note entering his voice at her hesitation.

'A bit,' she answered warily.

'Then we'll stop at a nice little pub I know down the road,' he said calmly, 'and you can tell me what you've been doing with yourself for the last ten years.'

She opened her mouth to make an objection, caught the hard set of his profile and the narrowed eyes, and changed her mind, settling back in her seat without a word. It would be too ridiculous to protest and somehow she didn't want to. The scene in the car and the revelations about his father had upset her more than she had realised and she didn't have the strength to oppose him, for the moment. She didn't doubt for an instant that he had spoken the truth, although she found the facts hard to equate with the mild, generous father-figure she had always known.

The pub was situated on a lonely stretch of road, sheltered by low, rolling hills behind and two enormous old gnarled oaks either side. It looked like a huge, sprawling cottage, roofed with mossy and lichened slates, diamond-leaded windows winking in the dusk of the dying day. 'The Old Man'. She looked at the creaking sign over the arched front door. 'He doesn't look very happy, does he?'

Cameron glanced up at the wizened, dour old man the sign portrayed. 'Perhaps he had woman trouble too,' he said drily as he took her arm and ushered her into the warmth. The interior was as enchanting as only an English country inn could be. A huge, crackling log fire with a massive dark oak mantelpiece took up most of one wall, the dark wood beams overhead and the copper and brass hanging in gleaming and careless profusion adding to the dateless charm of the place.

'Good evening, sir...' The innkeeper's voice faded as he peered closer in the dim light. 'Good grief, it's Cameron, isn't it? Cameron Strythe.'

'Hello, George.' Cameron shook the proferred hand warmly. 'It's been a long time; I wondered if you'd still be here.'

'You know me, Cam; they'll carry me out feet-first,' the middle-aged plump man returned cheerfully. 'It must be ten years since I saw you last.'

'About that,' Cameron returned easily, turning to Candy and drawing her forward. 'Meet Candy, George, and we'd love two halves of your draught cider. Best in the country,' he added in an aside to Candy. She stared at him, too surprised by yet another facet of his complex personality to speak. For the first time the harsh cynicism that was etched into each line of his hard, good-looking face had faded and she could almost imagine it was the old Cameron who was standing there. He seemed inordinately pleased that the publican had remembered him and, despite her misgivings, Candy couldn't stop a little dart of sympathy from softening her eyes.

'Did you miss England very much, Cam?' It was the first time she had used his nickname and she was unaware she had done so until his steel-blue eyes shot to hers, narrowing for a moment at the expression on her face.

'Feeling sorry for me, carrot-tops?' he asked laconically, raising a taunting eyebrow as the hardness she was used to returned to his face. 'There's no need; I'm a big boy now, or perhaps you hadn't noticed?' He was being deliberately hostile and she sensed that pity was repugnant to him and this was his way of covering it up, but in spite of that a small flame of anger swept through her, turning her brown eyes black.

'I can't imagine anyone feeling sorry for you,' she returned smartly, her eyes shooting daggers. 'You are the most unpleasant individual——'

'That's better.' He was smiling with acid mockery as the publican gave them two foaming glasses of the light-coloured cider, his eyes grey in the subdued lighting. 'Do you still do that wonderful steak and kidney pie, George?' he asked as he paid for the drinks. 'I've tasted that in my dreams for years.'

'There's not much changes round here, Cam,' the big man replied easily. 'For two, is it?'

'Candy?' Cameron turned an enquiring eyebrow to her. 'Would you like to see the menu?'

'Steak and kidney pie will do me fine, thanks.' She smiled at George, and as the inn-keeper made to move away he stopped and peered at her more closely. 'I'm sorry, miss, but you remind me of someone and I can't quite make out who,' he said slowly. 'This can't be the lady who used to come —— '

He had been speaking to Cameron, who interrupted firmly, his eyes cool. 'The lady who used to accompany me was Candy's sister, George, her big sister.' He smiled without it reaching his eyes. 'We never got married after all.'

'Oh, I see.' The publican looked acutely uncomfortable. 'I hope I didn't put my foot in it, Cam; I didn't mean ——'

'No problem.' Cameron moved off the bar stool and indicated a table for two in the corner by the fire. 'We'll eat there, I think, George, and two more ciders with the meal.'

As Candy followed him across the room she was conscious that although her legs were moving her mind remained stunned in over-drive. This had been his local with Michelle! They had clearly been favourites with the landlord and he had known they were en-gaged, and in spite of all that Cameron had the cheek to bring her here! He must have known the landlord would make some comment; he had done it on purpose to em-barrass her.

The turmoil inside her was reflected in her eyes as she sat down, spilling her drink as she slammed it abruptly on the table.

'I didn't think he would remember.' Cameron didn't try to pretend as he looked at her white face. 'It was a long time ago, after all.'

'It seems like yesterday to me,' she said quietly, a harsh brittleness in her voice as she forced herself to remain calm.

'Well, that's your problem, Candy, isn't it?' His voice was soft and for a moment the impact of his words didn't reach her shattered defences, and then as the realisation hit home she raised huge, stricken eyes to his watchful face.

'You just don't care, do you?' She was beyond feeling rage or anger, but there was a slow, painful ache that made breathing difficult tightening her chest. 'You don't care about anyone or anything. You're a dead man, Cameron, a walking dead man, without an iota of normal compassion or tenderness. I don't know why I thought I hated you, because there is nothing there to hate.' She had wanted to hurt him, wanted to lash out and pay him back for his coldness, but nothing had prepared her for the shock that met her eyes as for a brief, imperceptible moment the mask was ripped aside and she saw the real man staring out with raw, naked hurt turning his eyes brilliant. It was gone in an instant, but she felt sick with reaction, stumbling to her feet with a muttered excuse about the ladies' room.

Once in the tiny room she leant against the cold white-washed wall with a small exclamation of pain. What had he turned her into? She didn't recognise herself any more. She had never consciously tried to hurt anyone in her life and she couldn't believe she had just been so cruel. She raised a weary hand to her brow, pushing back her hair from her forehead. This whole thing was beyond her comprehension and she was sick of feeling so confused, so vulnerable, so angry...

When she walked back into the main room her eyes were drawn immediately to Cameron's bowed dark head as he sat staring down into his drink, and the knot in her stomach tightened. As she reached his side he looked up, his face expressionless, and she sank into her seat quickly. 'I'm sorry, Cam,' she said slowly. 'That was cruel and unnecessary.'

He stared at her for a full minute without speaking, his piercing blue eyes shuttered and distant, and then nodded quietly with a small smile. 'Stop looking so tragic, Candy; I've survived worse.' She blinked away the tears that were hovering at the back of her eyes and he suddenly reached forward, touching her cheek with his hand before leaning back again in his seat. 'It's all right, really.'

The moment of tenderness, so unexpected and surprising, was nearly her undoing, and she gulped at her drink frantically, finishing the glass before she realised what she had done, just as George brought two steaming plates to their table.

Let me just get through the rest of this evening and get home, she prayed silently as they ate, concentrating desperately on her food. He had awakened emotions in her that she didn't dream she was capable of feeling, and one thing was certain: she must never put herself in the position of being alone with him again. She disliked him, she was mistrustful of him, but there was something else gnawing away at her and she wouldn't take the lid off that particular Pandora's box and peer inside. She suddenly knew, with deep and utter conviction, that if she valued her peace of mind she would lock that box up and throw away the key for all time.

CHAPTER FOUR

'CAM'S on the phone. He said something about a dinner party?' Her mother popped her head round the kitchen door, where Candy was busy loading the washing-machine with muddy, wet clothes. She had been on a long, exhilarating walk with Jasper in the hills until darkness had driven them home, both covered in mud and wet to the skin. There had been total silence from Cameron for the last three days and, try as she might, he hadn't been out of her thoughts for a more than a minute until at last, utterly infuriated with herself, she had called Jasper and determined to walk the irritation and anger out of her system. It had worked—that was, until she had heard the phone ring.

'Oh, yes?' She kept her voice purposely casual as she closed the round glass door with a click, pressing the start button on the automatic machine and washing her dirty hands before following her mother out into the hall.

'Hello?' She was pleased her voice was firm and strong as she spoke into the receiver, despite her legs having developed the consistency of melted jelly.

'Candy?' The quiet voice was deep and penetrating and for a moment it was as though Cameron were in the room with her. 'You haven't forgotten I need you at the house tomorrow evening?'

That was just like him, she thought furiously. No pretending, no 'how are you?' or any time wasted on good manners. Just straight in with the curt orders again as though she were a servant or something. 'No, but I was hoping you had.' She didn't try to make her voice pleasant and there was screaming silence for a few seconds.

'I'll ignore that,' he barked tightly. 'Be ready for seven.'

'Yes, sir!' She answered in military style and again there was a pregnant pause before his voice sounded once more, intense irritation throbbing in its dark depths.

'Give it a rest, Candy,' he said wearily. 'It's like a confrontation with an armed missile every time we talk.'

'Oh, that's what we're doing, are we?' she answered quickly. 'Funny, but I had the impression you were giving the orders and I was waiting in line to receive them.'

'I see.' She heard him sigh audibly. 'And will it make any difference if I ask you to come?'

'You could try.'

'Yes, I could,' he answered wryly, 'and get told to go to hell for my pains? Am I right?'

'Dead right,' she said coolly.

'I thought so.' There was that grating quality in his voice now that told her he was hanging on to his temper with extreme difficulty. 'As I said, I'll call for you at seven.'

'I would prefer to make my own way, thank you.'

He swore, softly and vehemently, although the sound was muffled and she guessed he had his hand over the receiver. 'Crawl if you want to.' Now his voice held the texture of polished steel. 'But be there!' She heard the receiver slammed into place and, although her stomach was churning as she quietly hung up, she felt a moment's satisfaction that she had got under his skin. That was one battle he hadn't won; now on with the war!

'You look absolutely gorgeous.' Her mother sighed appreciatively at the slender, tall figure swathed in green silk as Candy collected her car keys from the coffee-table where she had slung them when arriving home from work. 'Doesn't she, Ernest?'

'Very nice.' Her father dismissed the beautiful green cocktail dress that had cost two weeks' salary and the carefully cultivated hair-do and looked at her pale, strained face instead, adding perceptively, 'A lamb to the slaughter?' He had always been able to read her mind ever since she was an infant on his knee. 'Cam's friends still perform the normal functions the rest of us do, love; they're merely a bit better off than most.'

'I know.' She nodded quickly, averting her eyes, relieved her parents had mistaken the anxiety she hadn't been able to hide for simple nerves. If they had been curious about her acceptance of Cameron's 'invitation' they hadn't mentioned it, for which she was supremely grateful. She never found it easy to lie and in this case she would have to have made a very good job of it.

The night was clear and cold and for once her little Mini behaved perfectly, starting first time. The short journey gave her time to marshall her defences and gain much-needed composure and she was glad she had arranged to drive herself. Driving always gave her a sense of her own worth: there was something immensely satisfying about being in sole charge of what was essentially a loaded weapon and handling it properly.

'Oh, Miss Candy, you do look lovely.' Mrs Baines peered at her from the lighted hallway. 'I hardly recognised you.' Candy took the backhanded compliment as it was meant and smiled, in spite of the enormous butterflies that had raced about her stomach on catching sight of the huge array of large and very expensive cars parked in the drive. Her little Mini had looked quite incongruous tucked between a stately Bentley and long, sleek Ferrari, and for a moment the impulse to turn and creep away had been paramount. Then a pair of very sharp and cold blue eyes had flashed into her mind and she had squared her shoulders resignedly. She would never give him that satisfaction, never!

'Good evening, Candy.' The deep, cool voice behind her made her swing round as she went to enter the drawing-room. Cameron was standing at the foot of the stairs, having just left his study, the ice-blue of his eyes in stark contrast to the darkly tanned skin. 'You're late.'

She felt the familiar anger sweep over her at his curt tone and flushed hotly. 'Yes, I know.' She made no effort to excuse herself; it had been deliberate and he knew it.

'I had thought in view of the fact that you know no one it would have been easier to be here when they all arrived, but no matter.' He waved a hand dismissively, his eyes hard on her face.

'Oh, I see,' she said sarcastically. 'The seven o'clock command was for *my* benefit?' She moved slightly and the green silk that was moulding her body like a second skin gleamed in the artificial light. Cameron's mouth tightened as his eyes narrowed, and there was an expression on his face that she couldn't read as he turned away, taking her arm in his.

'It's a pity that David isn't here to see you tonight,' he said blandly as they walked through the open doorway into the throng of people that seemed to fill the large room. 'You look stunning.' She glanced up at him quickly, detecting what was almost a note of censure in his voice. 'Not at all like the windswept maiden of our first meeting.'

'I hardly think a duffel coat and wellington boots would be appropriate tonight, do you?' she answered drily. 'And please leave David out of this.'

'Gladly.'

She stopped suddenly and Cameron stepped back a pace to join her, his face expressing the annoyance that was almost habitual when he looked at her. 'Now what?' he asked resignedly as he saw her gazing across the room.

'Isn't that Katherine Hamilton?' she asked in amazement. 'The actress?'

'Yes,' he answered shortly, his gaze flickering to join hers on the tall, willowy, beautiful blonde. 'She's an old friend.'

'She is?' Candy knew her voice was a squeak, but she couldn't hide her amazement. 'She's one person I admire tremendously. The work she's done for the wildlife trust is magnificent.'

'Kate is certainly more than a pretty face,' Cameron said slowly, 'but if you scratch beneath the surface most people are different from what you would expect.' He looked down at her with a harshly cynical twist to his mouth. 'Me, for instance.'

She wanted to make a tart, throw-away comment, but there was a strangely speculative quality in his face that caused her to drop her eyes instead, unsure of her ground.

'What? No quick, biting repartee?' he said softly.

'Now is not the time for childish indulgences,' she said swiftly and then flushed angrily as he gave a low, deep chuckle of genuine amusement.

'You'll be the death of me yet, Candy,' he said slowly as his eyes stroked over her hot face, his expression changing as a tall, beautifully dressed woman appeared at his side, her dark eyes in striking contrast to her exquisitely coiffured grey hair.

'Now how do I know this is Candy?' The woman was in her late fifties, but still quite remarkably attractive, with the sort of bone structure that was ageless. 'You are, aren't you?' she added urgently as neither Cameron nor Candy replied.

'It's all right, Monica, you haven't dropped one of your famous clangers,' Cameron said with quiet amusement as the silence lengthened. 'Monica Hardwick, meet Candy Baker.'

'Hi.' There was something very warm and natural in the beautiful face looking into hers and Candy found herself smiling back just as warmly. 'I've been dying to meet you.'

'Meet me?' Candy shook her head slightly. 'I think there's some mistake; you must have the wrong —— '

'Monica is the family solicitor, Candy; I've mentioned the school situation to her,' Cameron said smoothly as he put an arm round both their waists, effectively separating them from further conversation. 'Now, I'm sure both you ladies are in need of a cocktail before dinner; shall we...?'

The rest of the evening progressed in a confused blur of racy chit-chat, 'in' jokes and somewhat dubious gossip, all of which left

Candy with an aching jaw at having to keep her fixed smile in place. Dinner proved to be an oasis in the desert, seated as she was between Monica and her husband, with Cameron directly opposite. The three were obviously old friends and Candy found their easy banter restful to listen to, besides being immensely entertaining. She discovered Cameron had a dry, roguish sense of humour that she secretly had to admit was very like her own, frequently holding himself up to deliberate ridicule and laughing uproariously when Monica or Bill came in with a sly gibe. This slant on the man she was determined to hate was as unwelcome as it was confusing and she left the table with her mind buzzing and her head whirling.

'Come and talk to me,' Monica invited cheerfully as a long, slim redhead entwined herself round Bill and dragged him off to the other side of the room. Candy caught the despairing appeal in the glance he threw over his shoulder at his wife and couldn't repress a delighted giggle escaping her lips. 'Serves him right,' Monica said comfortably as she drew Candy over towards the wide window-seat, patting the space beside her as she pulled the curtain round in a semi-arc. 'He hates these sort of dos, always leaves me to do all the talking. We can be quiet here for a minute; all that lot are too busy trying to impress each other to notice we're missing.'

Candy stared at the elegant, beautiful woman looking at her so interestedly and smiled uncertainly. 'You're not at all as you look, are you, Monica? You seem quite different from the rest of the people here.'

'Thank goodness for that.' Monica breathed thankfully. 'If I thought I had settled into their mould I'd seriously consider finishing it all.' She paused. 'Although one or two are good types—Katherine Hamilton, for instance, and that little Pete Bales. He was with Cam on the oil-rigs, you know.'

'Was he?' Candy didn't quite know if she wanted to discuss Cameron with anyone and certainly not with someone who obviously held him in such esteem. 'You're very fond of Cameron, aren't you?'

'Yes, I am.' Monica looked her straight in the face and her expression was deadly serious now. 'He's the son Bill and I never had, and besides that he's a very good man, Candy.'

Now it was Candy's turn to be direct. She couldn't pretend to approve of Cameron and she suddenly felt that Monica wouldn't expect her to be anything less than honest. 'Perhaps you've seen a different side to him from the one I have,' she answered quietly, a hardness that the other woman noticed immediately coming into her eyes.

'Maybe.' Monica shrugged without taking her eyes off Candy's face. 'But I know the real Cam, the one underneath the mask. You were very fond of Charles, weren't you?' The question, coming out of nowhere, surprised Candy, and for a second she stared at Monica, sensing the quietly spoken words held more than the face content.

'He was very good to me and my family,' Candy said quietly, and Monica nodded slowly, her face troubled.

'Yes, he could be generous and kind, but there was a side to him that I suspect you never saw. He was very like Cam; he only showed you what he wanted you to see.' She shook her head contemplatively. 'When I took

over from my father as the Strythe family solicitor a lot of things fell into place that had
puzzled me for years. I had only known
Charles as my father's friend till then.' She
looked hard at Candy now. 'I said Cam was
like his father and that's true except for one
thing. Charles showed his good side to the
world and he could be a devil in private. More
often than not it's the other way round with
Cam.'

'Look, I don't think——' Candy shifted
uneasily as Monica cut her off with a raised
hand.

'I'm not trying to be unpleasant for the sake
of it, Candy, but if you want to understand
Cam there are things you should know.'
Candy looked at her in horror. The last thing
she wanted to do was to *understand* Cameron!
Monica seemed to have quite the wrong impression of their relationship.

'From when he was a very small child
Cam's life was made a misery by his father,'
Monica said quietly. 'Not in any physical
sense, and perhaps Charles never intended to
be cruel, but Cam was ignored at best and
often ridiculed unmercifully. I remember an

instance when I was here with my father when Cam was about ten.'

'Please, Monica...' Candy made to stand up, but Monica caught her hand urgently, her face unflinchingly determined.

'Cam had found a rabbit in the woods that was hurt, a broken leg or some such thing. He asked Charles if he could take it to the vet's.' She shook her head, her eyes going inward, and Candy sank back into her seat in spite of herself. She knew she wasn't going to like what she heard, but there was an invisible cord holding her in place now. 'Cam's always been crazy about animals; I think he transferred all the love he couldn't give to them.' Monica looked up from her murmuring and held Candy's wide brown gaze with her own. 'Charles disposed of the rabbit—I'm not sure how; I didn't want to know, frankly—but then he gave Cam a real dressing down in front of us all. Said he would never be a farmer, that he wasn't fit to run this place when he was older, that he was weak and spineless and so on.'

'What did Cam do?' Candy whispered faintly, her imagination feeding her a picture that was vivid in its painfulness.

'He took it as always,' Monica said slowly. 'Stood there until Charles had finished and then left without a word. He was more of a man at ten than Charles ever was. Charles mistook compassion for weakness. I confess I didn't like the man.'

'But Cam was going to shoot my dog.' She stared at Monica distractedly. 'He had a gun; he was going to shoot Jasper.'

'Cam, shoot anything? Never!' Monica looked at her in disgust. 'Don't you know him better than that? He does what he has to to keep the vermin down and such like, but to actually kill someone's pet?' She peered closer into Candy's white face. 'He's a strange man, I admit, and difficult to get close to, but if anyone ever did the rewards would be phenomenal. Do you know how he feels about —— ?'

'I wondered where you'd got to.' As Cameron's deep voice cut off Monica's whisper like a sharp axe both women shot round to see him standing to one side of the curtain, his eyes piercingly cold. 'Having a little tête-à-tête, Monica?' His icy blue gaze said something to the other woman that Candy couldn't read and Monica rose swiftly, patting Candy's hand as she left.

'I must rescue Bill from that redhead...' She was gone before Candy could react. Candy stiffened noticeably as Cameron eased himself down beside her, drawing the heavy velvet curtain right across the alcove, effectively shutting them off in their own private little world.

'And what were you and Monica talking about in such a cosy little huddle?' His voice was cold and tight and after one glance at his set face Candy kept her eyes on the carpet.

'Nothing much.' Her heart was jerking so badly that she felt quite light-headed. He looked fiercely handsome in the black dinner suit and snow-white shirt, his big, powerful body accentuated by the formal clothes and a fatal charm emanating from him that was all the more insidious for being totally natural. She suddenly felt he was as deep and unfathomable as one of space's black holes and a thousand times more dangerous. What did she really know about him? Very little, except that he was capable of great cruelty, as the affair with Michelle had borne out. That much was certain; the rest was a huge question mark.

'Nothing much.' He repeated her words in cold mockery, his face sardonic. 'I take it you have no intention of telling me the details of this "nothing much".'

'There's nothing to tell.' She looked him straight in the face now, her eyes shadowed. 'I told you, it was——'

'Nothing much. Yes, so you did.' His cool affrontery combined with an air of arrogant dominance hit the fire button and she stood up, anger bringing flaring colour into her face.

'Now look here, you, I didn't come here to be cross-questioned on everything I talk about, and if you think——'

'Look here, you?' He pulled her back down on the seat abruptly before she could move and kept one firm hand on her arm as he spoke. 'Is that the sort of English you teach the infants, Candy? Poor little kiddies...' His voice was low and taunting and there was dark satisfaction in his face as she spluttered for words, her rage effectively robbing her of coherent speech. 'You look quite beautiful to-night.' Now her lack of breath was caused by a different sensation as she was held by his eyes, devoid now of any mockery. 'Quite beautiful...'

'Don't...' Her voice was lost against his lips as he drew her into him, one hand tangling in the upswept silk of her hair as he leant over her on the broad seat. 'No...'

As his mouth opened above hers he took her lips in a kiss that began a fire in her very bones, the intoxicating smell of him filling her nostrils and sending her pulse racing in an orgy of delight. She felt as though she were melting into nothing as his hands moved down to her hips, travelling over her body in light, sensual exploration before returning to hold her face as he took her mouth in a deeper, probing caress that seemed to draw the very core of her into him.

As before, the will to resist had disappeared the moment his flesh had touched hers, but this time a small, untouched part of her remained lucid, aware that the physical sensations she was enjoying would soon be replaced by bitter, self-recriminating disgust.

'Leave me alone!' The sudden fierce push caught him totally by surprise and he would have fallen, perched as he was on the very edge of the seat, but for the animal-sharp reflexes that seemed an integral part of him. 'Get away from me!' Her voice, low and hard, hissed with furious outrage, and he caught her wrists in a steel hold as she twisted and turned against him.

'Calm down, you little wildcat.' His eyes were brilliant with anger and there was controlled violence in his hands as he forced her to sit quietly on the soft, padded seat. 'What's the matter with you, girl? I was only kissing you. Anyone would think——'

'I don't want you to kiss me; I don't even want you to touch me. You disgust me, Cameron Strythe; I find you repugnant——'

'Will you shut up, for crying out loud? You're going to be the cabaret for the evening at this rate.' He cast a glance over his shoulder at a sudden crescendo of sound behind the curtain, relaxing slightly as the noise continued at an almost deafening level.

As she sank back against the seat, her fury spent, he shook his head slowly. 'You can't fool me, you know, Candy.'

'What?' She stared at him, her velvet brown eyes huge in her heart-shaped face.

'You respond to me like a beautifully trained dog at its master's call. You might not like it, but you can't help it.'

'You arrogant, conceited —— '

'Do you want me to tell you how I know? Apart from the obvious signs, of course...' His mocking gaze swept over her and she was mortified to find the thin silk of her dress had done nothing to hide the results of his love-making, her breasts straining against the flimsy cloth, their points hard. 'Because I feel the same.' She looked up sharply then, her eyes narrowed. 'In the lines of the old saying, "We could make beautiful music together", Candy.'

'And after the musicians have put away their instruments?' She glared at him, her voice tight with bitterness. 'I've seen how you treat women who are stupid enough to fall in love with you, Cameron, and Michelle is living proof, isn't she? You might not like it, but Jamie exists. He is a person; you can't pretend he never happened.'

'Oh, I know what happened all right.' There was a dark grimness to his face now that sent a flicker of fear down her spine. She thought she had seen him in all his moods, but this expression was new to her; pure, cold, hard hatred. 'If anyone does, I do; believe me, Candy.' He stood up abruptly, his eyes like ice. 'One thing your sister did for me was to teach me that if you want something you take it, that number one comes first. I learnt the lesson well and I've lived the last ten years by its rules. I probably have a lot to thank Michelle for.' He paused and looked at her white, puzzled face with a bitter twist to his mouth. 'It's made me what I am today, after all—rich and successful. What more could you ask a woman for?'

'You talk as though you were the injured party,' Candy said faintly, the venom in his eyes piercing her anger and letting it trickle away, to be replaced by confused darkness. 'What about Michelle?'

'Michelle?' The name curled on his lips. 'Michelle doesn't exist.' He wrenched the curtain aside and left without another word, leaving her pale and shaking on the seat as she tried to bring some sense to what had transpired. The deeper she got into this, the less she understood it, and she bitterly resented the doubts he was putting into her mind. He was ruthless and selfish and hard and she wouldn't trust a word he said, or the insinuations he left unsaid. He was clever, too clever by half. She shook her head slowly. But could someone act so well? There had been something in his face when he had mentioned her sister's name that had chilled her blood.

'You aren't still sitting here?' Monica's bright voice brought her head up with a little jerk and she saw Bill was firmly attached to her arm. 'Come and join the party; if we have to suffer, so can you.'

The next few hours sped by, helped along by several glasses of wine and a long chat with Katherine Hamilton that was the one bright spot in otherwise meaningless chatter. As one or two of the guests began to drift away Cameron beckoned her abruptly to his side from the other side of the room. He had summoned her in such a fashion more than once as the night had progressed and her temper, never slow to rise, had been kept at simmering temperature all evening.

'You stay with me now until they've all gone,' he muttered in an undertone as she reached his side, his voice brusque. 'Do you understand?'

'Yes, master.' The enraged sparkle in her eyes belied the flatness of her voice and he glanced down at her as she positioned herself a few inches from his side.

'And at least look as though you want to be here. Put your arm through mine.'

'We aren't fooling anyone, you know,' she said tersely as she obeyed him reluctantly, the feel of the hard, firm body next to hers causing a little shiver to snake down her back. 'We aren't exactly love's young dream.'

'The crowd here tonight aren't exactly connoisseurs of human nature, Candy, or hadn't you noticed?' he asked drily as he looked down at her with that strange look in his eyes. 'You have served a purpose and kept the more predatory females away at the same time as acting as my hostess. That was all I required of you.'

'I'd have thought a man like you would want——'

She stopped as he raised her chin with one hand and she saw the look in his eyes. 'A man like me? What do you know of a man like me?' His voice was calm, almost conversational, but she knew he was annoyed by the metallic glitter in those windows to the soul. 'Do you think we had a harem on the oil-rigs for the use thereof or that there was an abundance of female company on my ranch in Australia? Wrong on both counts.' He dropped his hand to his side and looked straight ahead as he continued talking. 'I'm not the original Don Juan, whatever you may think.'

'And I suppose you haven't messed around in the last ten years?' she asked acidly, directing her gaze across the room as she spoke.

'I've been with men who work hard and play hard and I've done the same,' he said shortly. 'If you are asking me if I've had women then the answer is yes. "Messed around" is not quite how I would have described it, but, nevertheless, yes.'

'Oh.' She suddenly felt as though she had been punched hard in the stomach and something must have registered in her voice because he glanced down at her, his face sombre.

'I'm a man, Candy, not a monk. I don't suppose you're exactly a Vestal virgin.' She made no comment and his gaze sharpened as he took in the sudden flush in her cheeks. 'Hell, I didn't mean that the way it sounded; it's nothing to do with me. Your love life is your own business —— '

'It's kind of you to notice,' she said with deep sarcasm. 'If I had slept with half the men in Devon it's entirely my own concern.'

'With a surname like Baker that wouldn't surprise me in the least,' he returned coldly, his bitter expression fading as Katherine Hamilton reached their side, saying her goodbyes in that throaty, sensual voice that had captivated half of America. Candy answered the lovely actress automatically, her brain dissecting Cameron's last words, but the opportunity to ask him to explain himself was lost as more and more guests followed Katherine until only Monica and Bill were left.

'It's been lovely, Cam.' Monica placed a light kiss on Cameron's lips, touching his cheek gently as she did so. 'And I'm so pleased we've met you, Candy.'

'Thank you.' Candy smiled bewilderedly, surprised and a little dismayed at the older woman's enthusiasm. She really must set Monica right as soon as she could regarding her relationship with Cameron, but then she might never meet her again. That thought was soon shattered.

'Candy and I would like you to join us for Sunday lunch, if that's convenient?' Cameron kept his eyes on Monica as he spoke, but Candy's arm was suddenly pressed into his side in an iron lock and she recognised the silent warning, biting her lips in an effort to stop the exclamation that was hovering from escaping. 'Mrs Baines would like the opportunity to cook for more than one and Candy would hate me to eat alone on only my second Sunday home. Wouldn't you, sweetheart?' The last word was said lightly, but with unmistakable possessiveness, and for a moment the temptation to bite back was almost overwhelming. Then Kevin's small face shot before her and she remembered the threat hanging over the school, not to mention her father's livelihood.

'We'd love you to come.' Candy looked directly at Monica as she spoke, ignoring the tall figure at her side. 'It would make all the difference.'

'Would it?' Monica looked somewhat surprised at Candy's vehemence, but Candy sensed the insult had been recognised and accepted by Cameron's slight stiffening. 'That would be lovely, then, about twelve?'

'Fine.' Candy was annoyed to hear a slight throb of amusement in Cameron's dark voice as he made his farewells. So he thought all this was an entertaining game, did he?

'I thought tonight was going to be a one-off.' She went straight into the attack as Monica and Bill's little sports car disappeared down the drive.

'Did you?' He turned to look at her at the same moment as the moon scudded out from behind black clouds, turning his eyes to silver. 'Whyever did you think that?'

'Probably because I thought even you wouldn't be such a rat as to continue what is essentially blackmail.' She had no idea how the moonlight was stroking the dark red of her hair into glorious life, catching the little tendrils that had come adrift during the night and softening the deep velvety blackness of her eyes. 'I should have known, shouldn't I!'

'Yes, you should have, but then there is so much that you close your eyes to, isn't there? And such beautiful eyes, too.' She jerked away from him angrily as he went to touch her hair, and his face tightened, the faint smile on his lips dying. 'I haven't got an infectious disease, Candy.'

'That could only be an improvement on what you *have* got,' she said bitterly. 'I hate you, Cameron Strythe, I really do.'

'Now I'm beginning to find that refrain a little tiring,' he said slowly, and as a sudden gust of wind made her shiver he took her arm and led her back into the wide hall, shutting the heavy oak door quietly. 'Can we just take it as read that I appreciate your revulsion and leave it at that?' He was so infuriatingly cool, so untouched by any emotion that she could have screamed from pure frustration.

'As long as you do,' she flashed violently.

'Oh, I do.' He stood looking down at her, his face curiously remote. 'You're a constant little thing, aren't you, but it's sad when such loyalty is misplaced.'

'Look, Cameron —— '

'I am looking.' There was a thickness to his voice now and this time the shiver that snaked down her spine had nothing to do with the chill outside. He seemed overpoweringly large in the dim glow from the one light burning at the end of the hall, large and dangerously handsome. The dark, aloof aura that surrounded him in the day was more pronounced now, his eyes glittering and the tanned face imperturbable. She wondered what had happened in the last ten years to make him into the man he was now. He frightened her! The thought hit her consciousness and caused her eyes to dilate with shock. But not in the normal way. In a way that she couldn't even begin to understand herself, except that it touched something so deep inside her that she felt he reached her very core.

'I'm going.' She looked round wildly for her coat and he moved into the small cloakroom without speaking, returning immediately with it draped over his arm, his eyes hooded.

'Would you like me to drive you?' he asked coolly.

'No!' She recognised the note of panic in her voice and took a deep breath, forcing her voice into calm, modulated tones. 'No, thank you. I came in the Mini; it's somewhere out there...' She gestured vacantly, and a small smile touched the severe line of his mouth.

'I'm aware of that, but you had several glasses of wine during the evening.' She hadn't realised he had been watching her so closely and the knowledge brought hot colour into her cheeks. 'As a responsible schoolteacher who needs to set an example, I really think you should let me take you home.'

She knew he was mocking her and yet his words had brought a stab of guilt. She despised the casual drinker who ignored the drink and drive laws and yet here she was contemplating doing the very same thing. It just hadn't occurred to her, and now he was taking great satisfaction in pointing out her lack of thought.

'Thank you,' she said tightly. 'I presume you're OK to drive.'

'Two glasses of wine during the whole evening,' he returned easily. 'Alcohol has never been a source of stimulation with me.' There was something wicked in his eyes that caused the colour that had subsided to leap into furious life again, and as she turned for him to help her on with her coat she realised she was trembling. This was ridiculous! She gritted her teeth angrily. She had always been slightly irritated by women who suffered from 'nerves', and here she was acting like the original neurotic female of a million and one male jokes. It had to stop! No way was she going to countenance this.

There was the crystal-clear bite of frost in the air as they walked over to Cameron's Lamborghini, which was waiting to one side of the sweeping drive like a crouching animal under the star-studded sky. Some distance away her Mini, tiny and forlorn, looked like a small, abandoned puppy, and as she sank into the soft leather of the beautifully upholstered car she felt for a moment that it was symbolic of everything that had happened since Cameron's abrupt return into her life. She pulled her coat tightly around her and fastened her seatbelt silently, her face grim. Wealth and power were terrible weapons.

'You'll have lines before you're thirty.' As the engine purred into life she glanced at him by her side, his firm brown hands on the wheel and his eyes intent on the view ahead.

'What?'

'Frowning like that. You are the most disagreeable female I've met in a long time. Don't you ever try to charm the man you're with? You can take honesty too far, you know.' His voice was mockingly sardonic and as always he touched a raw spot, causing her eyes to sparkle and her mouth to straighten into a tight line.

'I wouldn't try to charm you if you were the last man on earth,' she said furiously. 'You're——'

'Don't start that again.' He sighed with mocking severity. 'I thought we had agreed that I'm fully acquainted with your feelings about me.' His voice was deep with hidden amusement.

'Oh, shut up!' She settled into her seat with her eyes blazing and her body taut, hearing his small chuckle of laughter with mixed feelings. He was impossible, absolutely impossible!

She was home in a matter of minutes and as the sleek car cruised to a halt at the top of the short drive she made to open the door. 'Hang on a moment, I don't want you accusing me of ungentlemanly behaviour, do I?' He was out of the car before she could voice the scathing reply hovering on her lips, opening the car door with an exaggerated flourish that added to her irritation.

'Sunday at twelve, then?' He took a step back, his eyes cool.

She looked up into his waiting face, her dark eyes mutinous. 'I have no choice, do I?' She paused and then couldn't resist voicing her displeasure. 'You had no right to put me in such an embarrassing position, Cameron. You knew if you asked Monica and Bill like that I would have no option but to go along with it.'

'Exactly.' He was quite unrepentant, leaning casually against the side of the car, the gleaming metal shining darkly in the moonlight.

'There must be hundreds of girls you could ask to have lunch with you; why pick on me?' There was puzzlement as well as rage in her voice and his eyes narrowed as he looked into her small, angry face.

'Oh, hundreds...' he agreed lightly, pausing as his expression changed and a shadow darkened the piercing cold eyes. 'Maybe I felt lonely for the old days—who knows?' It wasn't the whole truth, she could sense it, but suddenly the aura of icy remoteness that hung about him was lifted for a second and she knew instinctively that the first part of the sentence was true. He was lonely! He was more lonely than any human being should be; there was a dark fortress surrounding him, hard and strong.

'Yes...well...' She was out of her depth as the revelation touched something painful inside her. 'You should have asked,' she finished weakly.

'We both know what the answer would have been, don't we?' he replied slowly as a smile touched his mouth with fleeting irony. He thrust his hands deep into his pockets and turned from her, his eyes hard and iceberg-blue, leaving her standing uncertainly at the bottom of the steps leading to the front door.

'Cameron!' He turned by the door of the car, his face expressionless. 'What did you mean when you said you wouldn't be surprised what I'd done with a surname like Baker?' The gibe had been taunting her every moment since it was uttered.

He stood absolutely still, tall and big and dark in the dim light as the trees overhanging the drive waved their bare branches in the wind and somewhere in the distance a solitary dog barked mournfully into the blackness. 'You're a big girl now, Candy; you work it out.' His gaze was searingly sharp as they stood with their eyes locked over the distance separating them and she could no more have spoken than flown.

She shivered convulsively and pulled her coat tighter around her, knowing all the time that the chill came from within, not without. 'Look into yourself, Candy, be brave.' His voice was quiet and steady, but there was something throbbing in its deep softness that

was more menacingly unsettling than anything that had gone before. 'To really understand who you are you have to understand
others and that means taking the rose-
coloured glasses off at times, however painful.
Loving someone *in spite* of what they are is
true greatness and few of us rise to it; it's more
comfortable not to.'

'I don't wear rose-coloured glasses.' The
protest was without conviction and he shifted
slightly, opening the door of the car with his
eyes remaining locked on hers.

'That's for you to decide.' There was a
flatness in his voice that frightened her; it was
more of a challenge than any open accu-
sation. He eased himself into the car and
drove slowly down the drive without looking
at her again, and she stood in the cold
darkness until the sound of the engine had
faded into the night.

The dog was still barking, the sound
changing to deep-throated howls that matched
an ache deep inside her chest, and she only
moved when the biting cold of the March
night penetrated her coat and the thin ma-

terial of the cocktail dress, reminding her that she was half frozen.

'Why did you have to come back, Cameron Strythe?' she asked the emptiness around her as she climbed the steps to the house wearily, her high heels tapping an echoing blankness in the dark neutrality of the night. He was making her feel things she didn't want to feel, begin to question long-buried doubts that had no place in resurrection if she valued her peace of mind. And then there was the raw need that she had sensed in him more than once, however much he tried to hide it. That hurt her. She didn't know why it hurt, but it did, badly.

'I won't think about all this; I can't.' Even as she voiced the protest into the cold darkness her mind acknowledged that she was merely postponing the inevitable, but she shook her head determinedly, refusing to accept the insight in Cameron's words. She wouldn't let him intrude into her safe little world with his ogre of candour and the searing monster of honesty. She didn't realise until weeks later, when it was too late, that in her heart of hearts she had already admitted the truth.

CHAPTER FIVE

'WHAT made you decide to become a solicitor, Monica?' Sunday lunch had been a somewhat subdued affair, despite Candy's efforts to pretend that she was there by choice, and, as they had relaxed with coffee in the luxury of the drawing-room, Cameron's suggestion that they go for a walk had been eagerly approved by all present.

'I don't think I ever had any choice, really,' Monica answered with a wry twist to her mouth. 'Dad had hoped for a son to carry on the family business when I was born and when it became apparent there would be no more children and he was stuck with me he began an indoctrination programme to further his own ends. I didn't mind.' She smiled at Candy, pausing to stroke one of Cameron's black Labradors, which had come bounding to their side, eyes bright and black fur gleaming in the mild sunlight. As the dog raced off to join the two men several yards in front Monica slipped an arm casually through Candy's as they began to walk on again. 'I love my job—I can't imagine doing anything else—and as we can't have children I suppose it's become something of my baby, too.' Candy nodded slowly, but didn't question the last statement, sensing that although Monica had spoken quite naturally the subject was painful.

''lo, Miss.' She had almost stepped on Kevin, hidden as the small boy was in the thick, spiky, coarse grass that covered the rolling valley.

'Kevin!' She looked down at the little grubby face in surprise. 'You aren't here by yourself, are you?'

'No, miss.' He stood up reluctantly and immediately there was a whoop of delight from some thick undergrowth a few yards away and three more children sprang into view.

'Seen ya, Kev, seen ya. Ya didn't make the checkpoint!'

'We're playing armies, miss,' Kevin explained resignedly. 'It was my turn to get to the enemy camp without being seen, but...'

His voice trailed away and Candy smiled understandingly.

'But I spoilt it? Sorry, Kevin, I didn't know.'

'That's all right, miss,' the small boy said cheerfully, returning her smile brightly. 'I don't mind.'

'Hello, Miss Baker.' Julie Roberts appeared as if by magic by Candy's side now and Monica looked round with an exclamation of surprise.

'How many more of these little imps are there?'

'I've no idea.' Candy laughed. 'They do have a way of multiplying.'

'You needn't worry about Kevin, miss; I'm looking after him,' Julie said importantly, drawing herself up to her full three and a half feet, her thin, short plaits bobbing. 'He's had dinner at my house today, haven't you, Kevin?' She always spoke to Kevin as though he were years younger than herself instead of a few weeks, but Kevin seemed to like it, drawing from Julie's over-abundant stock of confidence gratefully. The two were inseparable and Candy had been very thankful for Julie's devotion since the accident.

'That's all right, then, Julie,' she replied warmly, smiling down at the small rosy-cheeked girl as she patted the top of Kevin's head. 'If Kevin's with you I know he's fine.'

The two ran off to join the other older children standing some distance away, Julie's high, shrill voice filtering back on the crisp air. 'Isn't Miss Baker lovely, Kevin, and didn't she look nice today?'

Candy's cheeks were pink as she turned to Monica to find the older woman looking at her thoughtfully.

'They love you, don't they?'

'Well, Kevin's been going through something of a rough patch over the last few weeks and I've put in more time with him than usual, and as Julie is his other half I guess it's inevitable we've got close.' The men had stopped some hundred yards or so in front and Cameron's deep voice cut through the air authoritatively.

'Come on, you two! You're making hard work of this.'

Monica waved the two of them on as she and Candy started walking again, and now her brow wrinkled as she spoke. 'Kevin? Is that the little boy who lost his father recently?'

'Yes.' Candy's voice was tight, partly with irritation at Cameron's autocratic command and partly with the pity that always consumed her when she saw the child. He seemed even more pathetic today, his face alight at being included in such a grown-up game with the others, and his thin little legs with their knobbly knees ending in enormous boots that were at least a couple of sizes too big for him. Candy knew his mother was struggling to clothe and feed them both and her anger boiled hot against Cameron. He could have made things better financially without even noticing it.

'I bet his mother thanks her lucky stars that she's been dealing with Cameron and not some stiff, white-collared employer who couldn't care less.'

'What?' Candy turned sharply to the other woman as Monica's words penetrated her own bitter thoughts. 'What do you mean?'

'Well, it's not everyone who would have been so generous, is it?' Monica's easy expression died as she saw the blank amazement on Candy's face. 'Oh, hell, you don't know,' she said flatly. 'This is the second time I've put my foot in it with you; Cameron's going to look for a new solicitor if I'm not careful. I just thought because you are so involved in the situation...' Her voice died away and she shook her head slowly. 'Oh, Monica, you never learn, do you?'

'Monica, if you don't tell me what you're talking about I'm going to scream,' Candy said urgently. The two men were making for the little pub in the next village just visible over the fields and had obviously given up on the women, striding ahead now with the dogs leaping by their sides.

'I shouldn't have said anything,' Monica began weakly, but Candy wasn't going to let her off the hook that easily.

'Well, you did, didn't you?' She put a comforting hand on Monica's arm. 'I promise I won't say anything to Cam, but I want to know.' It was strange, but in Monica's company the old nickname fell easily from her lips.

Monica nodded uneasily. 'Well...' She glanced across the wide expanse in front of them to where the two men were no more than small doll-type figures now in the distance. 'Cam came to see me when he first got back, before he even came to the house. He wanted to know how things stood and so on. I don't think he expected Charles to leave everything to him, you know...' Candy nodded thoughtfully. She was beginning to.

'Anyway, he sat looking through the sheaves of paper and so on, and he came to the business about Kevin's father. Charles had instructed me to pay the family off with a small goodwill sum, but Cam wasn't having any of that. Apparently he had known Mike, the father, said he was amazed he had reached the age he did in view of his drink problem.' She glanced at Candy, listening intently at her side. 'He said Meg, the mother, had had a rotten deal out of life so far and he didn't see why the boy should inherit the sins of the father. He instructed me to make an immediate lump-sum payment to cover all debts and set them up with a nice healthy bank balance, and also to organise a monthly allowance until either Meg marries again or Kevin reaches the age of sixteen. That's it.' She looked at Candy's stricken face thoughtfully. 'Aren't you pleased?'

'Yes,' said Candy weakly, staring at Monica with wide, horrified eyes.

'You don't look it.' Monica's voice held a note of concern. 'What's the matter, Candy?'

'I accused Cam of writing Kevin and his mother off,' Candy admitted slowly, 'in no uncertain terms, too.'

'Oh...' Monica expelled a deep, long breath. 'I can imagine how that went down.' Candy looked at her miserably, her red hair a mass of fire in the light from the dying sun, making her white face even paler in comparison. 'Well, it's his fault,' the older woman continued firmly. 'Don't look so tragic. He should have told you, especially when he thinks so much...' She stopped abruptly. 'Anyway, he should have told you.'

'He didn't have to,' Candy said quietly. 'I shouldn't have jumped to conclusions, should

I? But he seemed so cold when he talked about them.'

'Cam is the last person to wear his heart on his sleeve; you should know that,' Monica said mildly. 'But perhaps that's the trouble,' she continued thoughtfully. 'You don't know that, do you? You really don't know Cam at all.'

Candy stopped and stared at her silently, her brown eyes enormous in her pale face. 'I don't, do I?' She was speaking as if to herself and Monica was wise enough not to press the moment, walking on slowly until Candy joined her.

By the time they reached the quaint timber-framed seventeenth-century pub Candy had recovered both her colour and her voice, keeping up bright conversation with Monica and Bill while her mind raced and her eyes avoided Cameron's watchful gaze.

It was dusk when they emerged from the warmth of the pub into the sharply cold air, and Cameron suggested they take the route home through the village and on to the main road into the next village, the dogs falling into their place two steps behind him without needing to be told.

Lights were already glowing behind closed curtains as they wandered down the wide main street of colour-washed and timbered houses, past a row of pollarded trees and on to a smaller narrow path that led into the main unlit road connecting the two villages. A single solitary star shone in the brilliantly clear sky above and the air was spicy with the tang of frost and the faint smell of woodsmoke.

'I should think you're exhausted.' Cameron had tucked her arm through his, his sheepskin jacket making him seem even larger than normal, having let the other two walk on some way in front. 'This wonderful act that you've put on all evening has certainly worn me out, anyway.'

'I don't know what you mean,' she said in the bright, brittle voice she had used all evening, her facial muscles aching with the effort it had taken to keep smiling when she had never felt more like crying in all her life. 'I've had a lovely time.'

'You've had a lovely time?' he murmured disbelievingly, with a suspicion of laughter in his voice. 'Now that confirms it if nothing else.'

'Confirms what?' She forgot to pretend and glared at him angrily, noting as she did so that small laughter-lines stretched fan-wise from his eyes and that his mouth was curiously tender.

'Confirms that somewhere on that walk Monica said something that touched that soft heart of yours. What was it? Tales of me as a poor little lost infant frightened of the bogeyman? Whatever it was, you've avoided my eyes all night and been less than your normal vitriolic self.'

'You cheeky hound!' She tried to wrench her arm from his, but his touch tightened into hard steel as he looked down at her, open laughter in his face now.

'That's better,' he said comfortably as they continued walking along the narrow footpath bordering the road on one side and dark fields on the other. 'I know where I am when you're sending curses in my direction. You had me worried back there for a time.' There was an element in the deep voice she couldn't read, something important, but as the two in front called back to them the moment was lost and she concentrated on the walk home and the tremors in her stomach his nearness was causing. There was something intoxicating in walking with him like this, surrounded by intimate darkness and close to his side, and even as she tried to make her mind a blank and ignore the messages her body was sending in hot waves she knew she was fighting a losing battle. She had never met a man who attracted her like this one and she hated herself and him even more for exposing her weakness.

'Candy?' The deep voice intruding into her thoughts was soft and she raised reluctant eyes to meet his piercing blue gaze.

'Yes?' Her voice was wary.

'It doesn't have to be like this, you know. We were friends once; we could be again.'

'Never,' she said flatly, her voice firm. 'Those days are gone for ever.'

'Maybe you're right,' he said slowly as his eyes narrowed and his mouth took on the cynical twist she was used to. 'You aren't the lovable little kid sister any more and I'm not the devoted fiancé. We're both older and wiser.'

The moon was a bright white ball in the blue-black sky and now a million tiny stars had joined that first solitary leader, their sparkling, magical display catching Candy's heart as she looked upwards into the crisp, frosty air. She wanted something, something indefinable, with a hard, painful ache that had grown over the last few days but had been there, muted down and silent, for a long, long time. Ten long years, in fact.

She had missed him! The revelation was shocking in its abruptness and caused her steps to falter as she shivered suddenly. No! She hadn't, she hadn't! She wouldn't let it be true.

'Cold?' He had mistaken her shudder for something else and she nodded quickly, pulling her arm from his and sticking her hands in the deep fur-lined pockets of her coat.

'A little.' She kept her eyes straight ahead.

'We'll soon be home and a nice hot toddy will set you to rights.' He put a casual arm around her shoulders and she forced herself not to jerk away. Control, control, Candy, she thought resolutely; it's all a matter of control.

'I thought I might as well drop off home on the way, actually,' she said quietly. 'We pass my door walking this way.'

'No way, sweetheart.' There was granite in the deep voice now and the arm round her shoulders became a subtle warning. 'You'll see it through to the bitter end.'

'As you like.' She was pleased her voice sounded so casual; he would never know the effort it involved. 'I just thought —— '

'I know exactly what you thought.' They had reached the outskirts of the village now and Monica and Bill were waiting for them at one side of the widening path. 'You are nothing if not transparent.'

She glared at him angrily, her eyes stormy, and he smiled coldly. 'You don't like that? Sorry, kiddo.' He was being deliberately cruel and it took all her will-power to school her face into blandness as they reached the others. 'Candy's longing for a hot toddy; how about you two?'

She saw Monica cast a shrewd glance at her set face, but Bill smiled amiably, his rotund face beaming. 'Don't mind if I do, Cam! Not for Monica, though. She lost the toss; she's driving.' Monica's attention was switched back to her husband as she stuck out her tongue at his smiling face with a childish gesture of irritation.

'Always the same,' she said resignedly as they tramped the last few hundred yards home. 'Men have a way of always coming up trumps, don't they?' But her eyes were loving on Bill's plump face.

'And how!' Candy's exclamation had more fervour than tact and although Cameron passed the moment off with some laughing comment she knew Monica's eyes were tight on her again as they reached the long wind-swept drive, and that Cameron's gaze had more than a touch of ice in its blue depths.

Well, so what? she thought defiantly. I'm blowed if he's having it all his own way!

After a game of cards that should have been hilarious and probably was for everyone else but Candy, and two rounds of Cameron's hot, steaming punch, Monica and Bill finally stood up to leave. 'Can we give you a lift, Candy? You didn't come in your car, did you?'

Monica asked as the four of them walked into the wide, panelled hallway, the rosy glow from an old antique oil lamp the only illumination in the shadowed darkness. Cameron had explained earlier that one of the concessions to modern living that grated on him was the harsh brightness of electric light and, although in total agreement, Candy would rather have died than admit it. Now she was glad of the dim light as she replied to Monica's offer.

'I've got my old bike outside, actually, so no, thanks, a spot of exercise will take off a few of that punch's calories.'

'You came on your bike?' Monica's voice was a mild shriek of delight and she cast an amused glance at Cameron, whose implacable features were giving nothing away.

'Nothing to do with me, Monica.' His voice was a lazy drawl, but Candy knew he was displeased as his eyes swept over her flushed face in one piercing glance. 'I offered to pick Candy up, but she assured me she was making her own way here. I must admit the mode of transport has surprised me too.' After a few more laughing, bantering comments that

Candy did her best to cope with, Monica and Bill left, and immediately their car disappeared down the drive Candy turned and stepped into the hall, flicking her coat off a chair by the entrance, where she had left it earlier.

'I'll be off, then.' She didn't look up as she spoke, but was aware of every muscle in his big body as he moved to stand silently by her side.

'Very clever, Candy.' To anyone else the quiet, even tone would have been deceptive, but she caught the thread of cold steel and forced her eyes to meet his, her face defiant.

'What?' She faced him, her hair a deep, glowing chestnut-red in the soft light and her eyes pools of blackness.

'The little manoeuvre with the bike. In view of last time you weren't risking driving, were you?'

'I don't know what you mean,' she said coldly as her stomach trembled. 'I fancied a bike ride; is that a crime?'

'Rubbish.' He eyed her cynically. 'Too bad you didn't know Monica and Bill would offer you a lift, but I can understand you couldn't rely on that eventuality. The risk was too great, wasn't it? You might have had, horror of horrors, to allow me to take you home again.'

'Now it's you who's talking rubbish,' she declared as firmly as her clenched stomach muscles would allow. 'You really have no idea —— '

'On the contrary, my fiery little vixen, I have a very good idea.' He lifted a strand of silky hair as he spoke and let it slowly drift through his fingers, his eyes thoughtful. 'I have the idea that you daren't trust yourself to let me drive you home. That you don't trust yourself to be alone with me.'

'Well, full marks for conceit, Cameron,' she said coolly as hot anger quenched the trembling and turned her eyes blazing. 'Go to the top of the class.'

'I intend to.' He smiled slowly, although it didn't reach those deadly blue eyes. 'You didn't want a quiet tête-à-tête here, just the two of us, alone, did you?' There was a biting contempt in his voice now, along with something else, a derision that licked along her anger, igniting fresh fires. 'Do you really think

I'm going to leap on you like some demented animal? Is that what you think?'

'I wouldn't put anything past you, Cameron,' she snapped furiously. 'Anything at all.'

'That is perfectly obvious.' He folded his arms and leant back against the wall and now she couldn't define the look on his face. 'You can't run from me forever, Candy; there's nowhere to hide.'

'The rest of my life wouldn't be long enough,' she said bitterly as their eyes locked. 'You might have a certain basic appeal, Cameron, but as far as I'm concerned it's skin-deep.'

Now she knew she had got through to him as the dull red colour searing his high cheekbones turned his eyes brilliant, but when he spoke his voice was controlled and quiet, his body still relaxed. 'A certain basic appeal?' He let his eyes run insultingly over her slight figure in cynical appraisal. 'Well, that's a start, isn't it?'

'Not from where I'm standing.' She glared at him angrily and his face had a cruel chill as he moved towards her.

'Maybe you're standing in the wrong place.' As he pulled her towards him her mind registered that there was no gentleness in his actions like before, and that, humiliatingly, in spite of that her body thrilled at his touch as he crushed her against him. There was fear and anger in her stiffness as she fought against betraying herself, her lips firmly closed against his and her arms limp by her side. She would rather die than let him guess how much his touch meant to her.

The pressure of the hard, punishing kiss slackened as she didn't respond, and now his lips were gentle, teasing hers in such a sweet, tantalising caress that she found her hands were clenched fists by her sides as his hands moved in a slow, rhythmic massage over her back that was incredibly sensual. 'Relax ... don't fight it.'

Almost of their own volition her hands moved slowly up, over his taut, muscled arms and on to the broad masculine shoulders to rest in the warm hollow of his neck. 'Don't...' They both knew she didn't mean it and as he kept on kissing her, stroking her, she knew with a feeling of total panic that she was lost.

'There.' Amazingly, shockingly, he had moved her from him, and now he was standing in his original position, hard, lean body pressed nonchalantly against the wall as his cool blue gaze raked her hot face in calm, insolent scrutiny. 'A certain basic appeal? I can live with that.'

For a moment Candy felt that the punishment for her hot, furious words was more than she could bear and then her small chin came up in unconscious pride. He had broken her sister, but she would die before he broke her!

'Have you quite finished?' Her eyes were coal-black with hate as she stared into his hard face, and he looked at her for a long, still moment before he shook his head slightly, his expression unreadable.

'For now.'

'I can go, then?' she said tersely, with savage sarcasm.

'Of course.' He waved a casual hand towards the door. 'Whenever you like.' She had reached the door before he spoke again and his voice was still bland and calm. 'I suppose it wouldn't do any good at all to say I don't like the idea of you cycling home alone at this time of night, especially in view of the icy roads?'

She turned slowly, her eyes withering. 'No good at all.'

'I thought not.' He smiled slowly. 'You really are the most amazing female.'

'If that's supposed to be a compliment you can keep it,' she snapped furiously. 'I don't want —— '

'Enough.' He raised a laconic hand, but the expression in his eyes halted her words. 'Just one thing, Candy. Tonight I'll let it go, but in future I will collect you and take you home. Is that understood?'

'In future?' She stared at him in absolute amazement. 'You don't seriously think for one minute that I'm coming here again, do you? You might have got some sort of strange kick out of the travesty of the last few days, but I sure haven't. There is no way I'm becoming a doormat for you, Cameron Strythe, school or no school. You can take your threats and —— '

'I think I get the message without any embroidering, in spite of your eloquent way with words.' He was laughing at her again! She could see it in the darkness of those piercing eyes and the way he was trying to keep his mouth straight. He was actually laughing at her!

'Goodnight!' She flung herself down the steps, hearing his mocking chuckle as her teeth gritted helplessly. She would love to be a man for just sixty seconds and give him a good punch on the nose. The man was insufferable.

She knew he was standing watching her as she walked to her battered old bike, dropping her handbag into the small wicker basket fixed on to the handlebars with a small sigh as she turned the heavy, cumbersome frame round slowly.

'That looks more suitable for a museum than anything else,' the hated voice drawled slowly from the doorway. 'Can you actually ride that thing?'

She ignored him with magnificent disdain, wheeling the bike along the side of the house and on to the gravelled drive as though he weren't there. Just as she passed him she raised her head with a biting retort hovering on her lips, only for it to die as she saw the unguarded expression on his face seconds before a shutter came down and wiped it away.

They stared at each other for a long moment in the stark, cold beauty of the frosty night, and then she continued on her way without a backward glance at the tall, silent figure at the top of the steps silhouetted in the lighted doorway.

Once out of sight of the house in a curve in the drive she leant against the solid, comforting trunk of an old oak tree, her head spinning. She must have been mistaken! For a moment she had thought there was a raw hunger in that dark gaze that had matched the searing hurt that night in the pub after she had driven his car. It had been a trick of the light! As though to confirm that thought, the moon suddenly disappeared behind a solitary cloud, plunging the night into a mass of dancing shadows. Yes, she'd imagined it, imagined the pain.

'Come on, Candy, home, girl.' At the bottom of the drive she climbed on the bike carefully, aware that the roads were deceptively dark with black ice. Concentrating on getting home in one piece calmed her racing heart and stilled the trembling in her legs, but once in the warm comfort of her bed she lay staring at the starry sky through her window for hours as sleep remained irritatingly elusive.

'This is ridiculous!' At three o'clock, wide awake and thoroughly exasperated, she flung back the covers and marched downstairs, jerking the belt of her long, fluffy dressing-gown round her impatiently.

Slightly mollified by Jasper's ecstatic re-action to an unaccustomed night-time companion, she put a pot of coffee on to percolate, having totally given up on the idea of sleep. Jasper looked at her adoringly, his deep brown eyes as bright as buttons and his mouth smiling when she curled up on the settee with a mug in her hand, and, as she patted the sofa beside her, normally forbidden territory, he leapt up beside her quickly before she changed her mind.

'Oh, Jasper...' As his warm, soft body snuggled against her, his head resting puppy-fashion in her lap, she had an overwhelming urge to cry and cry against the silky fur. Everything had gone so wrong, but there was more to it than that . . . The image of a darkly tanned, brilliantly blue-eyed face swam before her and she bit her lip until she tasted blood. She would not allow herself to think . . . anything. She shook her head in the darkness. He was turning her world upside-down and it had to stop. No more blackmail, no more dinners, no more sly innuendos for her mind to toy with. 'That's it, Cameron Strythe.' Jasper looked up enquiringly as she spoke and at the surprised look on his face she felt the glimmer of a smile touch her lips. He must think she was mad, and maybe she had been for a while. But no more. Enough was enough.

She was on tenterhooks the next day, expecting a phone call, a knock on the door, but there was nothing. As one day followed another in an easy pattern she began to relax, hoping against hope that the cruel game was over and she would be left alone.

'Cam called today,' her mother said casually as she arrived home from work on Friday night, her arms stacked with grubby exercise books to mark. 'Wondered if you'd like to repeat last Sunday and have lunch with him again?'

'No can do.' Candy kept her face averted as she left the room. 'Masses to do. Be an angel and give him a ring for me and explain, would you? Thanks...' The invitation was repeated the following week after another seven days of silence and this time Candy phoned him herself to refuse, putting down the phone immediately after a few curt words before he had time to reply.

She couldn't quite understand why Cameron had called when he knew she would be at the school, but that evening her mother let slip that he was in the habit of popping in for a cup of tea on the odd afternoon. 'He just mentioned you might like to have lunch with him,' Vivien said uncomfortably as she stared at her daughter's glowering face, 'while he was here.'

'Am I the only normal one in this family?' They had been sitting in companionable silence in the lounge, her parents watching an old movie on television and Candy marking books in the corner, but now the air crackled with tension.

'What does that mean?' her father asked quietly, a frown wrinkling his brow at her tone.

'We're talking about Cameron, for goodness' sake!' She stared across the room at her parents in amazement. 'Cameron Strythe! Anyone would think he was the prodigal son instead of the biggest rat that ever drew breath. I don't understand you two, I really don't. You've welcomed him back with open arms after all he's done——'

'Don't be intolerant about what you don't know.' For a second she thought she had misheard her father's quiet voice, but then her mother put a hand on his arm, her voice anxious.

'Ernest.'

'Don't know?' She was beginning to feel that these two dear people whom she had been so close to for so long were strangers. 'I know enough. The man hasn't got a grain of natural human decency and nothing has been quite right since he came back.' She stood up quickly. 'I don't want to have a row with you, so let's leave it, shall we? Jasper needs a walk. I won't be long.'

When she came back an hour later everything seemed back to normal, but the conversation had left a question mark in her mind that she found hard to ignore. There were too many things that didn't add up, suddenly, and of all people she should know that two and two made four.

She purposely filled her weekend with a round of activity, spending the Saturday with an old friend in the next village and going to the cinema at night in the midst of a laughing, noisy crowd. Sunday morning dawned bright and warm, a quirk of nature so often found in English weather, producing a summer's day at the end of a bitingly cold, blustery March, and on a whim she loaded Jasper and a hastily prepared picnic in the back of her Mini and took off for the hills, travelling miles to find a small lake lost in surrounding, rolling countryside, where she spent a wonderful day without meeting a soul, tramping miles with Jasper at her side, returning to the car as dusk sent warning mauve shadows over the skyline.

It was only on the way home, as she felt an unfamiliar dread as they neared the village, that she was forced to admit to herself that she hadn't wanted to stay around in the one place she usually loved. She wouldn't let the phrase 'running away' remain in her mind for more than a second, banishing it along with all the doubts, but as she drew into the small drive and saw her home, silhouetted against a blazing sky of red, yellow and deep, fiery orange, she had the strangest feeling that maybe she wouldn't be seeing it for much longer. Because one thing was certain; the whole of Devon, let alone their small village, wouldn't be big enough to house Cameron and herself. If she lost this fight, unthinkable though it was, then she would be the one to have to leave.

CHAPTER SIX

'GOOD evening, Candy.' As she locked the heavy, arched oak door of the old school on Monday evening she knew she had been expecting this. It had been too much to hope that he would leave her alone. Fairy-tales were for children, after all.

She turned round slowly, her smile tight and her brown eyes wary. 'Hello, Cameron, what brings you this way?' If she had hoped to keep things casual that hope died as she saw the expression on his face.

'Oh, I just thought I'd have a wander through the village as it's such a wonderful evening,' he said sarcastically as the slow drizzle that had replaced yesterday's warmth intensified. 'What else?'

'If you're going to be unpleasant I've got better things to do than listen——' As she made to brush past him he seized her arm in a cruel grip, swinging her round to face him with such force that her words were cut off in mid-stream. 'Now look here——'

'I've no intention of looking anywhere but straight into your lovely, stubborn, obstinate face, Miss Baker.' His voice was cool and firm, but she sensed there was a fire burning somewhere inside, and he was hanging on to his temper with difficulty in spite of outward appearances. 'You are going to talk to me, whether you like it or not, and now!'

'And I suppose you're going to make me?' she asked sarcastically, jerking her arm free of his hand and flinging back a strand of silky red hair that had blown across her face.

'If I have to.' His voice was grim now and there was no vestige of softness in his face. 'I'm sick of you treating me as the village leper. You're making things difficult for everyone concerned, can't you see that?'

She stared at him in the dull light, the overcast grey sky above and misty, fine rain throwing the piercing blue of his eyes into dazzling prominence. They caught and held her, their power hypnotic. 'Look, Cameron——'

'No, you look, Candy!' The words were like pistol-shots and she jumped slightly, her eyes widening. 'I've had all I'm about to take from you so just, for once in your life, shut up and get into my car.'

'No way.' She shook her head, the tiny droplets of water like diamonds in the glowing red. 'I've no intention of going anywhere with you.'

'I just want to talk, damn it.' He glowered at her furiously. 'We can do it here, standing in the rain until we're both completely wet through, or we can behave like sensible, mature adults and sit in the dry. Obviously for one of us such an action would be completely out of character,' he finished with heavy sarcasm.

She hesitated, chewing her bottom lip uncomfortably. It was ridiculous when he put it like that, and already she could feel globules of cold water beginning to trickle down her neck and the chill of the evening penetrating her coat.

'Come on.' He took her silence as agreement and gripped her arm again, pulling her down the old stone steps and over the narrow country road to where the Lamborghini sat with stately disregard for the weather. 'Get in.' His tone was autocratic, firing her quick temper, but she bit back the retort that sprang to mind, sinking into the car's luxurious interior with a guilty feeling of pleasure. She hadn't been looking forward to the walk home, short though it was. Bright sunshine had bathed the lanes and meadows when she had woken that morning and foolishly she had thought it would last, deciding to leave the Mini tucked up in the garage.

'What do you want to talk about?' They had driven for some minutes in tense silence and Candy felt her nerves stretched to breaking-point, although Cameron seemed quite oblivious to her presence.

'In a moment.' He didn't look at her as he spoke, all his attention concentrated on the wet, winding road and hair-raising bends. Just when she thought she could bear it no longer he turned off the main road into a tiny, over-grown lane, bringing the car to a halt after a few yards in front of a ancient, dilapidated stile surrounded by dripping wet greenery.

'There's a wonderful walk down there on a summer's day,' he said conversationally as he cut the engine and settled back in his seat, indicating the rolling meadows and wooded hills beyond the car with a sweep of his hand.

She didn't answer for a long moment. It was raining in earnest now, the sound vibrating on the roof and a torrent of water effectively closing them in from the world outside. 'Well?' She looked at him coldly, her senses registering how good he looked while her mind warned her not to betray her thoughts for a second. 'You'd better get on with it; I've got a lot to do tonight.'

'That's an invitation no man could refuse.' Before she could gauge what he was about to do he had leaned across his seat in one swift movement, folding her into his arms with an expertise that was unmistakable, a wicked gleam in his eyes that spoke of inward amusement at her predicament.

'Let me go!' When she tried to pull away his arms tightened around her, crushing her even further into his hard body as he half lay across her. 'Let me go now!' Her eyes were blazing as they stared into his and now there was no vestige of humour in his eyes, but a dark, hot passion that met something deep inside her even as she tried to block what was happening out of her mind.

'Not yet.' His voice was a thick, husky whisper and as his lips travelled down the graceful curve of her neck to the beating pulse in the base of her throat she gave a long, soft moan in spite of herself. Desire was racing through her, white-hot and fierce, and she was helpless in the grip of an excitement that was alien.

His mouth searched for hers, claiming her lips in a long, deep, penetrating kiss that made her toes curl and her legs tremble, the blood singing in her ears in a wild frenzy. She had the strangest feeling that she had never been truly alive till this moment, that from this second on nothing would ever be the same again. She was aware that his hands were moving over her shaking body in a gentle caress, but she was beyond rational thought, each nerve-end gloriously alive and proving that she was tuned in to his need as though they were one.

'You see, you can't pretend...' There was a throbbing note of triumph in his voice that caught at the delirium that had possessed her, washing away the layers of madness until it was cold day again. 'You can't deny what's between us——'

She reared up so violently that she caught him totally by surprise, forcing him upwards in spite of his superior weight and size as she scrambled into an undignified kneeling position on her seat, her small face as white as a sheet except for two furious spots of colour on the top of her cheekbones. 'There's nothing between us, Cameron,' she hissed savagely. 'Nothing except years of betrayal and hate and misery. Do you really think I would be so insanely foolish as to let myself be persuaded to be another Michelle?'

He was frozen into a menacingly crouching position as he stared unblinkingly into her dark eyes, and as she watched the colour slowly drain from his face at her words she wondered, just for a fleeting moment of time, what she had done.

'By that you mean...?' he asked slowly, his voice expressionless.

'Pregnant and abandoned,' she said recklessly, a hot flush of colour staining her cheeks vivid pink.

'Pregnant and abandoned,' he repeated coldly as he settled back into his seat without taking his eyes from hers. 'Touching, very touching. Was that Michelle's version of the story?' His lips had curled scornfully over her sister's name and that fact alone gave her the courage to continue.

'I've never asked Michelle about that awful time,' she said tightly, her eyes fiery. 'She was going through hell and she didn't need her kid sister asking stupid questions, but everyone seemed to forget I was old enough to understand the birds and the bees. You used her, Cameron, and then walked away when things got too hot. I shall never forgive you, never.' There had been a touch of hysteria in the last words, but by comparison he was icy-cold, his eyes a glittering grey-blue as he looked her over from head to foot, his expression sardonic. 'What you did was unforgivable.'

'You have no idea what I did, just as you have no idea what Michelle was,' he said scathingly. 'You don't know her.'

'She's my sister!' she shot back wildly.

'She was a tramp.' His voice was cold with hate. 'If anyone was the innocent, I was. Your beloved sister was running around with half of —— '

As her hand made contact with the hard skin of his face she saw the blow register in the pearly blue of his eyes, but otherwise he was immobile, the bitter twist to his mouth and narrowed eyes seemingly frozen in time. She sank back in her seat, her breath coming in tiny, sobbing gasps, and for a moment all was quiet except for the steady beat of the rain outside.

'You're a fool, Candy.' Something had died in his voice as he stared at her, the misted windows drawing his face even closer. 'You've been blind for years. Go and see Michelle if you don't believe me. Talk to her, ask her what happened all those years ago, and then face the truth with the same guts you used to face me.'

'Never.' Her eyes were wide with the shock of all that had happened. 'I can't rake up all the pain for Michelle now; she's happy at last with a husband who adores her and a lovely home. Besides, there would be no point to it. I know what I know and nothing will convince me otherwise.'

A veil had come down over his face as she had been speaking, turning it into the hard, cynical mask he had been wearing that first day when she had met him again. There was no warmth, no tenderness in his eyes now, just a weary, resigned bitterness that seemed to have suddenly aged him ten years. 'You've made your choice; think what you like,' he said flatly as he started the engine again. 'Live in the past if the past is so precious to you, but I've finally realised I have to let it go. We're in different worlds, Candy, aeons apart.' She wanted to fight against what he was saying, to smash that dead look in his eyes, but there were no words she could use to reach him, because she was lost herself, lost in a confusion of searing memories and harsh pain that made her eyes blank and her mouth straight.

'Goodbye, Candy.' As he drew up outside her house she felt that the simple words were a portent for the future, but merely nodded a reply as she stumbled from the car, the falling rain hitting her face in pinpricks of icy numbness, bringing pain to her stiff features. He had turned the car and roared off before she had even inserted her key in the door, and for a moment she felt completely bereft, as though deprived of something essential to her existence.

'You're late.' Her mother was busy in the kitchen as she divested herself of her coat and shoes, going on her knees in front of the fire to give Jasper a cuddle, hiding her face in the protection of his thick fur as she heard her mother's padding footsteps come into the room.

'Sorry.' Her voice was muffled in the golden-white silk. 'Cameron picked me up; we needed to discuss a few things, the school and so on...' She sat up slowly, her hair a bright red tangle round her damp face. 'I've got a raging headache, actually; I think I'll have a lie-down for a bit. Don't keep dinner for me.'

'Candy?' She stopped in the doorway to the room at the sound of anxiety in her mother's voice. 'Is everything all right?'

'Fine.' She didn't turn round. Mothers were mothers the world over and she had never been able to fool hers for a minute. One look at her face and there would be a host of questions she was incapable of answering, especially right now. 'I'll probably be down later.'

After a hot, reviving shower she sat drying her hair in front of the window, dressed in her old dressing-gown, watching the story-book view in front of her shrouded in its deep, misty veil with unseeing eyes. Why was she feeling like this? As though there was something inside her that had been ripped out by the roots?

After a time she switched on her little portable TV, but was unable to concentrate, lying back on her bed with the headache she had professed fast becoming a reality.

'Candy?' She woke to a room filled with darkness, the television flickering its pictures into the blackness, the voices muted. 'I brought you a hot drink. How's the headache?'

'Better, I think.' She struggled into a sitting position as her mother switched on the bedside lamp, bathing the room in a warm rosy glow that was restful to the eyes. 'Thanks, you shouldn't have bothered.'

'No bother.' Her mother sat down on the side of the bed, her gentle eyes thoughtful as she peered into Candy's haunted eyes. 'Is it Cam? Have you fallen for him?'

The unexpected challenge took Candy completely by surprise, giving her no time to marshall her defences, and, as she stared aghast into the lined face watching her with such concern, it was as though the bottom of her world had just fallen out. Fallen for him? She hadn't fallen for him. She loved him with a consuming passion that had grown from childish, adolescent puppy love into the full-blown adult variety that would last a lifetime. Why hadn't she recognised it before? How could she have ignored what her heart had been telling her all along?

'No, of course not.' She realised she was staring vacantly at her mother as though she were an apparition and tried a weak smile that failed dismally. 'How could I? After what he did to Michelle and everything.'

'Forget Michelle!' her mother said impatiently as Candy stared at her in amazement. 'The past is past and you are the future. What's the matter with you, girl?' It was a watered-down version of her conversation with Cameron earlier, and for a second Candy felt she was going mad. 'You were only a child in those days, Candy,' her mother continued more gently. 'There were things that couldn't be explained at first and then it was too late. Life is never black and white, but all different shades of grey; things often aren't what they seem.'

'What are you saying?' Her mother's eyes dropped before the intensity of Candy's and she shook her head slowly.

'It's not for me to betray a confidence, and you know me better than to ask. Go and see Michelle, Candy, if Cameron means anything at all to you. Talk to her. Explain things to her. She's not your enemy.'

'I never thought she was,' Candy said in surprise. 'I just didn't want to upset her, after all this time ——'

'Candy, just think of yourself for once,' her mother said irritably. 'I've got one daughter who does nothing but that and the other one can't see the wood for the trees.' The conversation was becoming more like Alice in Wonderland every moment to Candy, and she shook her head slowly as her mother left the room with a light pat on her shoulder. The headache had returned with renewed vigour, which wasn't surprising in the circumstances.

She had never felt so totally confused and lost in her life. What was the matter with everyone? If anyone else told her things were not always as they seemed she would explode. And Cameron. Her heart stopped and then pounded painfully as she felt the strength drain from her limbs. How could she? How could she love him? But she did, totally, irrevocably and for ever. He was her pivot, the axis on which the world turned, fixed in the very centre of her heart and life.

'What am I going to do?' The empty room held no reply and she felt a sense of panic so severe that its violence made her feel sick. She loved a man who had left her sister expecting his baby without a backward glance, stayed away from his father and his home for ten years without a shred of remorse, and seemed to enjoy blackmailing her into a position of subservience every time they met to satisfy some weird whim of his own. And still she loved him.

After a restless night of tossing and turning she woke heavy-eyed and weary to face a damp, cold Tuesday morning in a building where the heating had broken down. She stuck it out till mid-morning, but when she noticed some of the children's fingers turning blue she made a few phone calls and arranged for everyone to be picked up, finding willing baby-sitters for those children whose parents were at work.

'Maybe Cameron's right after all?' she muttered grimly to herself as she kicked the old boiler viciously. 'Maybe this place should be closed down.'

Walking home through the village, her heart suddenly jumped into her mouth as she noticed a dark red car in the distance. It had to be him. The average daily wage around here couldn't even keep that monster in petrol.

'Hello, Candy. No school?' The car had been parked outside the local village shop that sold everything from hammers and nails to ice-cream, and as she walked gingerly into the bright, clean interior the familiar smell of home-cured bacon teased her nostrils. The small, elderly shopkeeper had greeted her loudly, but the tall dark figure standing with his back towards her, apparently engrossed in choosing a box of chocolates from the small display in front of him, didn't move a muscle.

'No.' Her eyes flickered to the stiff, taut back and then returned to Mr Miller's round red face. 'The boiler's broken down...again.' Turn round, Cameron, please, she thought painfully.

'Oh, well.' The shopkeeper smiled cheerfully. 'I suppose the bairns didn't object to an unexpected day's holiday. What can I get you?'

'Oh...' She glanced round quickly. 'A quarter of ham, please, off the bone.' She realised the palms of her hands were damp.

'Right you are.'

As Mr Miller went into the back of the shop, where he kept the cold meats and dairy produce, she took a deep breath and ventured to Cameron's side, rubbing her hands against her coat.

'Hello.' He turned at her voice and looked down at her, his eyes remote and his face unsmiling.

'Good morning, Candy.' She could have been a vague acquaintance who necessitated the minimum degree of politeness.

'I didn't know you liked chocolates.' Good grief, girl, she thought disgustedly, how pathetic; you can do better than that!

'They're for Mrs Baines. I discovered this morning it's her birthday.' He paused, his face set in austere lines. 'I'll get someone to call and fix the boiler this afternoon; the appropriate authorities will no doubt take forever.'

'Thank you.' She stared at him helplessly, seeing nothing but distant civility in the cold blue eyes. What could she say? What was there to say? Nothing had altered really, except that she had admitted her madness to herself.

As Mr Miller returned with the ham Cameron dropped a note on the counter, tucking the box of chocolates he had chosen under his arm. 'I think that covers it; put anything left over into the Sunday school outing fund for the kids.' He had gone before either of them could say a word, the door swinging shut behind him as the bell rang madly overhead, his face grim and strained.

'He's in a hurry,' Mr Miller remarked contentedly as he rang up the purchase on the huge, battered old till. 'Seems nice enough, though, but a bit aloof. Still, he always was a lonely kid, so I suppose that's inevitable.'

Candy heard the old man's words in the back of her mind, but all her senses were honed in on Cameron as he walked to the car. She saw him pause as he reached the long, low machine and straighten his shoulders wearily, as though the weight of some heavy burden was too much for him. The gesture hurt her unbearably, but then the next instant he had unlocked the car and dropped the chocolates into the back seat, folding himself into the vehicle and driving off without a glance in the direction of the shop.

'Here you are, then, Candy.' She turned slowly, her eyes vague and dazed as they glanced at the shopkeeper, and his expression straightened as he saw her pale face. 'Are you feeling all right, love? Want to sit down a minute? It's that school; the cold's got into you.'

'No, I'm fine, really.' She paid for the ham and then left without picking it up, retracing her steps with a wan smile as Mr Miller called to her from behind his counter.

'Best go home and have a hot drink,' he advised comfortingly. 'Nothing like a hot mug of milk with a touch of brandy in it for warming you up, I always say.'

She smiled without answering and left the shop quickly, knowing the coldness inside her could never be warmed by anything external. Something had crystallised in her in the last few minutes and now she knew with absolute certainty what she must do, what she should have done weeks ago.

She was relieved to find the house was empty when she reached home—her mother had obviously taken Jasper for a walk—and she wasted no time, not stopping even to divest herself of her coat before reaching for the phone.

'Hi, this is 496738.'

'Mellie?' For a moment Candy's courage almost deserted her and then she took a deep breath and carried on. 'It's Candy, Mellie; how are things?'

'Hi, Candy.' Her sister sounded delighted to hear from her, which made Candy feel thoroughly uncomfortable. 'What are you doing ringing at this time of the day?'

'The boiler again.' She heard her sister give a deep sigh and knew what was coming next.

'Why don't you leave that ghastly hole and get a decent job up here, for goodness' sake? You know you could live with us until you found a place, and Tim says your qualifications would get you a job anywhere. You're crazy, Candy, absolutely crazy.'

'Yes, well, be that as it may.' This was the same conversation that they had had a hundred times over, but today, heightened by emotion, it grated unbearably.

'You won't listen to reason, will you?' She could almost see Michelle's rosebud mouth pull tight and the long almond-shaped brown eyes harden. She knew her sister thought she was burying herself alive with her refusal to leave the village, but they had always wanted such different things out of life. She could accept that. Michelle couldn't.

'Look, can I come down and stay for a few days at Easter?' She spoke quickly before she changed her mind.

'Great!' There was a delighted shriek at the other end of the phone and she had to smile to herself at Michelle's enthusiasm. Her sister had notched this up as a small victory, a step in the right direction. She knew just how Michelle's mind worked.

They talked for another five minutes, Michelle describing in great detail her recent trip to Paris with Tim and their new car, and then Candy rang off, her mind whirling. Had she done the right thing? Was she going to stir up a hornet's nest and get badly stung in the process? She sighed wearily. She had to ask Michelle what had really happened all those years ago. She had to *know*.

Maybe it wouldn't do her any good. She ran a trembling hand across her brow and sighed deeply. Cameron had obviously had more than enough of her, as his attitude today had clearly shown, so why was she pursuing this? Why ask questions that by their very content would disturb and hurt Michelle when it was all past history, dead and gone? But it wasn't. She remembered the stoop to Cameron's shoulders and the downward curve of his head and her heart twisted again.

Her parents knew the truth. She suddenly felt it with absolute conviction. They knew something that enabled them to accept Cameron back into their lives without any re-criminations or bitterness.

She shut her eyes tightly for a moment and bit hard on her bottom lip. For better or worse, in ten days' time she would know the truth.

CHAPTER SEVEN

'YOU really have got the most beautiful home, Mellie.'

'I know.' Her sister's voice held immense satisfaction as she glanced round the immaculate kitchen with a small smile. They were sitting having morning coffee, perched on two breakfast stools that overlooked the pretty London garden, all shrubs, flowers and cane garden furniture with not a bird in sight. Michelle discouraged the birds in her garden. Messy things, she had told Candy with a small yawn.

'Don't you ever long for wide open spaces?' Candy asked quietly, glancing at the high brick walls surrounding the small garden.

'Me?' Michelle looked at her in horror. 'You must be joking. If I ever see another cow or horse in my life it will be too soon. I love city life. You would too if you gave it half a chance.' She flicked back her heavy blonde

187

hair that boasted of a wickedly expensive cut and slanted her heavily lashed eyes at Candy. 'What did you really come up for, Candy?'

'What?' Candy had forgotten those rare flashes of stark honesty that made up part of Michelle's complex personality. Most of the time her sister led her life on a very superficial level, careful never to delve too deep, but she was capable of great and surprising depths, as her utter devotion to her children showed. She adored each one of them, but Candy had noticed that there was a tenderness in her dealings with Jamie that was missing with the other two, as though she needed to make something up to him.

'You loathe it here, you know you do. It's lovely to have you, but I normally have to nag and nag for you to come. And you've been so withdrawn.'

'Have I?' Candy looked startled. Her sister was more perceptive than she would like at times. 'Sorry.'

'I get the awful feeling my time of reckoning has come. Am I right?' Michelle asked lightly with a wry grimace, but Candy noticed her eyes were dark with emotion. 'Cameron's back, isn't he?'

'Yes,' Candy admitted as hot colour seared her cheekbones, 'he's back.'

'And you like him.' It was said flatly with no emotion, more a statement of fact than a question.

'Look, Mellie, you don't have to discuss——'

'Oh, but I do, don't I?' Michelle's eyes had a hard glint in them now. 'What's he been saying about me?'

'Nothing much.' Candy looked hard at her sister now. 'But I owe it to him to ask you the truth, not just for him, Mellie, but for me. I want to know, to know...' She stopped and took a deep breath, uncertain of how to continue.

'He hasn't told you, then?' Michelle's face was pale now and her eyes shadowed. 'Really?'

'He's intimated things...' Candy gestured uncomfortably. 'Nothing definite, but he seems to bear you a grudge when it should be the other way round. Nothing seems to make sense.' She gazed at her sister appealingly. 'I'm not asking just for the sake of it, Mellie, believe me.'

'You love him?' There was an edge of pain in Michelle's voice that rasped against Candy's heart, and for a moment she wondered what on earth she was doing here, opening up old wounds. It was unforgivable. She should have known better. 'Do you, Candy?' Michelle was holding her now with her slanted eyes and Candy looked at her for a long moment before nodding slowly, her cheeks flushed.

'Yes, I love him,' she said painfully. 'He's the last person on this earth I should love, but I do.'

Michelle subsided on her stool, her taut body relaxing as she touched Candy's face lightly with her hand. 'Well, I think I'd better make some fresh coffee; we've got a lot of talking to do. Just one thing, Candy...' Candy looked up, surprised at the note of pleading in Michelle's voice; she had never heard it before. 'Don't hate me, will you? I couldn't bear it if you did.' The slanted eyes were luminous with unshed tears.

'Don't be so silly.' Candy reached across and gave her sister's slender body a swift hug. 'I could never do that.'

'Jamie isn't Cameron's son.' They had taken their fresh cup of coffee into Michelle's sparkling white-and-honey-coloured lounge, where lace curtains were moving gently in the breeze from the open windows, the beautifully warm April day filtering into the immaculate room carefully.

'He isn't?' Candy knew a moment's indescribable relief. 'But I thought——'

'I know what you thought.' Michelle dropped her eyes to the cup clasped in her hands, her heavy fold of hair falling across flushed cheeks. 'You were meant to think that, everyone was. I couldn't bear for anyone to know the truth then, to know...' She stopped and raised her eyes to Candy's intent face. 'There were several men who could have been Jamie's father,' she said simply.

'Mellie, what are you saying?' Candy asked softly. 'Why?'

'I wanted it all,' Michelle said quietly. 'I loved Cameron, in my fashion I *did* love him, but I wanted more. I was only just twenty-two, Candy; I felt I hadn't lived.' She moved restlessly in her seat and stood up, walking over to the window and gazing through the expensive lace. 'I needed excitement, intrigue; I wanted to know I could attract any man I desired.'

'And did you?' Candy wanted to go over and hug the stiff figure, but sat where she was.

'Too true,' Michelle said bitterly. 'I was such a fool. They only wanted one thing, but I was too caught up in myself to see that.'

'But if you don't know who the father was, how do you know it wasn't Cameron?' Candy asked slowly, her mind whirling.

'Because Cameron was the one man who didn't ask me to sleep with him,' Michelle said painfully. 'We were engaged to be married and he was content to wait. He respected me,' she said weakly. 'He didn't want to pressurise me into doing anything I might regret. He...' Her voice broke and she moved back to the chair, wiping her eyes with the back of her hand.

'Don't go on, Mellie,' Candy said quickly. 'It doesn't matter——'

'Of course it matters,' Michelle said fiercely. 'Every time I've thought of him in the last ten years I've seen his face that last night. He was devastated and yet I made him suffer still more by letting everyone think he was the father, just to cover my own back. I surprise myself, you know, Candy,' she said with a note of bewilderment in her voice, 'I really do.' She stared at Candy miserably. 'That night when I told him I was so brash, so confident. I told him if he really loved me he would stand by me and support me and the baby anyway. I said I didn't know who the father was, that it could have been one of several, that they didn't mean a thing and it was him I loved.'

'What did he say?' Candy whispered, her eyes on her sister's white face.

'He told me to go to hell,' Michelle said slowly. 'And then I threatened him. I said I would ruin his reputation, that everyone would believe me, that his father would make him marry me. And Uncle Charles tried.' She looked at Candy forlornly. 'He didn't listen to a word Cam said and they had a terrible row. That's when Cam left.'

'Oh, Mellie...' Candy looked at this sister she had always loved in spite of herself, and found she hadn't got the heart to condemn her out of hand. Michelle had suffered from her wildness, and she felt the burden of guilt Michelle had carried over the years had been a heavy one.

'Do Mum and Dad know the truth?' Candy asked quietly. 'Do they know Cameron isn't the father?'

'Yes, they know.' Michelle looked at her wretchedly. 'When Jamie was born, when I first saw his tiny face and held him, I knew I had to come clean. I'd been given such a gift, Candy, this tiny little person perfectly formed with all his toes and fingers, that I couldn't start off a new life without clearing things with the family. I knew it'd be difficult and it was—' her eyes narrowed in remembrance '—but I somehow felt that if I didn't try to put things right Jamie might be taken away from me. Silly, but that's how I felt.'

'And so?' Candy prompted softly.

'So I told Mum and Dad and Uncle Charles.'

'Uncle Charles? He knew? What did he say?' Candy asked in surprise.

'He wouldn't believe me at first.' Michelle's face twisted with remembered puzzlement. 'I couldn't understand him; I still don't. It was almost as though he wanted Cam to be guilty, as though it was important to him that Cam took the blame. Maybe he just wanted Jamie to be his grandchild, I don't know.'

'I don't think it was that,' Candy said slowly, her heart chilling at her sister's words.

'And it was Uncle Charles who insisted as few people be told as possible. He said they wouldn't believe it anyway and as I was leaving the district it was better just to let things die a natural death, not to rake it all up again. I have to admit I was only too pleased to agree with him at the time. Maybe that was wrong, I don't know,' she finished miserably.

'Did he tell Cameron you'd told the truth?'

'Yes.' Michelle nodded her blonde head definitively. 'Dad made sure of that. He and Uncle Charles actually went to see Cam, but Dad said it was a disaster. Uncle Charles was so weird, cold and unbending, and Cam seemed as though he had had enough of it all. I suppose he had,' she added reflectively.

'Poor Cameron...' Candy whispered sadly. 'He didn't have a soul in the world, did he?' Michelle twisted uncomfortably on her seat and fiddled awkwardly with her coffee-cup, her eyes lowered. 'Why didn't you tell me, though?' As the thought occurred to Candy she raised troubled brown eyes to Michelle's face. 'Why keep me in the dark?'

'You were only just thirteen when Jamie was born,' Michelle said defensively, 'and we weren't sure how much of it you had taken in, anyway. Uncle Charles said he didn't want you to know and Mum and Dad weren't sure; they said they'd leave it up to me one way or the other.'

'And you didn't want to tell me,' Candy said bleakly.

'Don't look like that, Candy,' Michelle said urgently as she saw the hurt in her sister's eyes. 'It wasn't like that, really. I suppose if you want the truth I just wanted someone in the family who was on my side. You'd always been such a pet to me and so fierce and protective once I was pregnant. Mum and Dad tried to pretend that they'd forgiven me, but I knew they hadn't really, not so much for getting pregnant, but for involving Cam, and then the confession about the other lads. Well, it was all too much for them, I guess. Things have never been the same again, anyway.'

'I see.' Candy rose and walked over to the window, gazing with unseeing eyes at the smart London street outside, its neat, clean paths and carefully planted trees in pristine order complementing the chic, elegant houses and modish cars parked strategically every few yards. She noticed the number of BMWs with wry cynicism. Yes, this whole scene was made for Michelle; it suited her perfectly. 'Does Tim know?'

'Of course.' Michelle rose gracefully and joined Candy at the window. 'Things are different up here, Candy. Tim didn't turn a hair; he'd seen it all before. Anyway, he could hardly have objected, considering the number of women he's had, and still has, if my suspicions are right.'

'And you don't mind?' Candy was appalled and it showed in every stretched feature of her face.

'Not really.' Michelle gave a laconic shrug to her slim shoulders. 'While the cat's away, you know... Tim has his fun; I have mine. It doesn't mean anything.'

'Mellie!' Candy stepped back a pace and stared into her sister's lovely face. 'Are you serious?'

'I told you, things are different here,' Michelle said irritably. 'Don't look at me like that! If it suits us both, so what?'

The return of the children from the park with Tim in tow abruptly ended further revelations, but that night, as Candy lay tossing and turning in the strange bed, she went over and over the conversation in her mind, becoming conscious of the inevitability of Michelle's words as she pondered them through the dark hours. She had known since that night after the dinner party! She sat up sharply in bed with a gesture of repudiation, but the truth was not to be banished so easily. She had known then, in her heart of hearts, that Cameron wasn't capable of the cruelty she had accused him of, but she had been too cowardly to face the consequences of following that thought through. He had been right. Taking off the rose-coloured glasses was painful, but not as painful as thinking about the torture his father had put him through from childhood right through to manhood. And Michelle's heartless betrayal would have hit him doubly hard. A lonely, loveless childhood and then such treachery by the one person he had pinned his hopes of the future on. How could he ever trust anyone again, believe in anyone?

The soft pink fingers of dawn were beginning to lighten the night sky when at last she fell into restless sleep, her mind made up. As soon as she got back home she would go and see Cameron, whether he wanted to see her or not. She owed it to him to apologise for how wrong she had been, how obstinately blind. It amazed her how he could bear to have anything to do with any of them; all the village and its inhabitants held for him were cold, dark memories of a time he would obviously prefer to forget. When she thought how she had treated him, the things she had said, she writhed about the bed in hot misery. He must hate her. He must really hate her.

'Candy! What are you doing here?' Surprise warred with wariness on Cameron's face as he stared down at her from the doorstep, and for a moment the surprise of seeing him when she had expected Mrs Baines to open the door robbed her of coherent speech. It didn't help that he was looking devastatingly attractive, his dark hair slicked back from his forehead, accentuating the vivid blue eyes, and his denim jeans hugging his hips in a way that brought sudden warmth to her cheeks. 'Is everything all right?' he asked urgently when she still didn't speak. 'There's nothing wrong with your father or Vivien?'

'No, no...' She waved her hand in a way that could have meant anything. 'Nothing's wrong, at least not like that. What I mean to say is...' She stopped abruptly. She had rehearsed this little speech every long minute of every long day she had spent at Michelle's, and now it had deserted her. He just looked so...good. How could she have been so stupid, so stubborn?

'Well, this is a first.' Amazingly he was smiling and she noticed for the first time, with a piercing pang to her heart, how his smile softened the harsh contours of his face and gave a light to his eyes that brought the young Cameron of ten years ago poignantly alive.

'A first?' She stared at him, bewildered.

'To see you lost for words. Normally I can't stop you talking.' He took her arm, drawing her into the house. 'And usually it doesn't bode well for me.'

'No.' She paused as they stood in the hall. 'Well, that's what I want to talk to you about. You see...' Her words trailed away as she heard the low murmur of voices from the drawing-room. 'Oh, I'm sorry. You have visitors?'

'Unfortunately, yes.' He was looking at her keenly, and she was suddenly very conscious of her flushed face and windswept hair. 'Pete Bales came down for a few days over Easter with a few friends. You remember Pete?'

'He worked with you on the oil-rigs?' Something ground hard inside her as she wondered if any females were included in the party.

'Yes.' He raked his hand through his hair and the movement made her hotly aware of his broad, muscled shoulders as they moved under the thin cotton of his shirt. 'There were a few of us who had always planned to meet up again and now seemed as good a time as any.'

'Oh.' It didn't sound as if any women were involved and she felt immensely relieved. 'I'll leave you to it, then.'

'Hang on a minute, Candy.' He took her arm again as she turned to leave and the warmth of his firm flesh seemed to burn her. He was so male. Every tissue, every fibre, dominantly male. 'They're going home today, as it happens. Have you got anything planned for this evening?'

'No.' She looked up into his dark face and was conscious that she was holding her breath with anticipation. That last time she had seen him, two weeks ago now, he had been so cold and withdrawn, so icily polite, but maybe he had missed her just a little? If only for the sparks they struck off each other?

'Would you like to go out for a meal?' He was treading carefully, very carefully, she could sense it.

'I'd love to,' she said simply and caught the flash of surprise that flared in his eyes for a second before he nodded with studied nonchalance.

'Good.' He smiled again and she caught her breath. How could she have not seen him for the man he was all those weeks ago? She had been such a fool. 'I'll pick you up at eight o'clock, OK?'

'OK.' She turned quickly towards the front door as the sound of men's laughter rose from the drawing-room and there was the sound of someone calling Cameron's name.

'Hey, Candy.' He stopped her for the second time and now wry humour was twisting that firm mouth and crinkling the vivid blue eyes. 'I said *I'll* pick *you* up at eight.'

'I heard you.' She knew what he meant, but was determined not to rise to the bait.

'My, my.' He leant back against the wall, folding his arms as he looked at her sardonically, a shaft of warm April sunlight picking out the faintest trace of blond highlights the severe cut hadn't completely been able to banish. 'Now I know there are fairies! Or maybe the magic of Easter has been able to soothe the savage breast?'

'Shut up, Cam,' she said flatly, and although she was unaware she had spoken the old nickname a quick narrowing of his eyes told her of her mistake.

'Do I detect a slight mellowing?' There was no laughter in his face now, just a tight intentness that unnerved her more than a little.

She was saved from having to make a reply as the drawing-room door opened with a swift flourish and Pete Bales stuck his head out, his expression changing as he saw the look on Cameron's face.

'Sorry, mate.' He raised an embarrassed hand to Candy and she raised her own in response. 'I thought you were talking to Mrs Baines.'

'She's out shopping,' Cameron said shortly without taking his eyes off Candy's hot face. 'I'll be back in a minute.'

'Fine, take your time, no hurry...' Pete's good-natured face was a bright shade of red as he closed the door, his voice unnaturally bright.

'I've really got to be going.' This time Candy made the door without further delay, closing it behind her quickly, conscious that Cameron was still standing pressed against the wall, every line of his big, long body still, as though he was waiting for something.

She walked down the sunlit drive in a daze, telling herself with every step that the invitation meant nothing, that he was just lonely and being kind, that she was any port in a storm, but, no matter how she tried, the swell of hope wouldn't be denied. She loved him! In spite of the ridiculousness of the old cliché she was aware that the grass was greener, the clear sky overhead bluer, the world altogether more beautiful since when she had walked this same route a few minutes before. He was taking her out tonight! She gave a little skip and then looked around quickly, her cheeks scarlet.

'Calm down, Candy, calm down.' She had never talked to herself so much as she had done in the last few weeks! Here she was, a mature schoolteacher approaching the age of twenty-three, and acting like a schoolgirl with a crush on the head teacher. But it wasn't a crush. And she wasn't a schoolgirl.

Her parents, bless them, had made no comment at all when she had told them of her dinner date, but when she disappeared up-stairs at five o'clock with a muttered explanation that she looked a mess and needed a bath, her mother had raised musing eyebrows. 'Half an hour and you're usually ready,' she said calmly. 'Still, you know best.'

Candy answered her with a weak smile and beat a hasty retreat to the bathroom, locking the door and subsiding into a long, hot, relaxing bath for nearly an hour. Her body and mind felt as if they belonged to her again as she stepped out of the soothing caress of the silky water some time later, and as she dried her hair and applied careful make-up she found herself humming in a way she hadn't done for weeks.

She opted for a look of smart casualness, teaming a cream cashmere dress with high-heeled shoes of the same shade and leaving her hair loose to soften the plainness of the dress, letting its silky red mass of burnished copper be her only adornment. She was ready long before eight, sitting at her window and watching the shades of dusk slowly turn the sky pewter-dark, purposely emptying her mind of any thought beyond that of appreciating the panoramic view spread out before her. She was going to be composed tonight, composed and tranquil, even if it killed her!

'Candy! Cam's here!' As her mother's voice filtered upstairs Candy took a deep breath and stood up slowly on legs that were annoyingly wobbly. She had heard his car purr scrunchily to a halt on the drive outside, heard the car door slam and the front doorbell ring, and then the deep, mellow tones of his dark voice speaking to her mother, but had been unable to move, a mixture of fear, wild hope and crippling shyness keeping her in her seat.

'You look...breathtakingly lovely.' He was standing in the hall at the bottom of the stairs as she left her bedroom, and as she walked down the stairs his eyes never left her for a second, the look on his face bringing the blood pounding in her ears and making her hands damp.

'Thank you. You look pretty good yourself,' she said lightly, willing her voice not to betray her. It was the second time she had seen him in a suit, the first being at the disastrous dinner party weeks before, and like then he looked stunning, the dark, tanned suit and deep blue eyes making her breath catch in her throat.

'Here.' She looked down in surprise and he pressed a small package into her hands, her eyes lighting up with pleasure as she saw the dark, exotic petals of the orchid through the transparent box. 'The red matches your hair,' he said softly as he took the flower from her, carefully fixing it on to the front of her dress, where it lay in magnificent contrast to the soft cream material.

'It's gorgeous, Cam, thank you.' Her mother had watched the little exchange with a studiously blank expression, but now a small smile clung to her lips as she handed Candy her jacket.

'Your father brought me a bunch of lupins he had taken from his mother's garden without her knowing on our first real date,' she said blithely, regardless of the innuendo. 'Carefully wrapped in the morning's newspaper. They were lovely, though...' She smiled at them both as her husband's voice sounded from the room beyond.

'You never told me you knew that!'

She smiled at them both warmly. 'You'd better go before I let any more cats out of the bag.'

The night was cool with just a slight bite in the air, and once in Cameron's car it was deliciously warm. 'Your parents are nice people.' His voice was quiet as he swung the powerful car out into the road after checking his mirrors and she nodded agreement.

'I know.'

'You're very lucky.' There was no bitterness or rancour in his voice, but, knowing what she did, her heart went out to him. 'I can see why you are so well-rounded as a person.'

'Well-rounded?' She pretended annoyance as she glanced down at her curves. 'Not too well-rounded, I hope?'

'You know what I mean.' A slight smile touched the severe line of his mouth. 'I wouldn't presume to criticise your figure. It's perfect, as I'm sure you've been told before?'

'Hundreds of times,' she agreed wickedly.

'How many hundreds?' He wasn't fooling now and she recognised instantly the question he was asking.

'I've never slept with a man before, Cam.' The car swerved slightly, but apart from that he betrayed no reaction to her quiet, steady voice, his eyes still intent on the dark, winding road before him, his hands gripping the wheel tightly. 'That's what you were asking, weren't you?' It was a calm, serene statement and he didn't deny it, his face impossible to read. Knowing what she did about him, she had sensed total honesty was vitally important. He could take the truth, whatever it had been; there was nothing small about this man. Duplicity was the only thing he couldn't handle.

'Unfortunately I have slept with several women, Candy.' His voice was devoid of emotion. 'In my defence I can only say that it was right at the time.'

'Then why ''unfortunately''?' she asked softly, forcing the pain from her voice with sheer will-power.

'Because now, at this moment in time, I realise I took their bodies without being prepared to make any real commitment to them. I never realised that before. Not until...' He stopped suddenly.

'Until?' she asked quietly.

'Later.' He had withdrawn from her again; she could sense it. 'We're nearly there.'

'There' turned out to be a perfectly wonderful restaurant attached to a sumptuous hotel nestling in its own magnificent grounds complete with a cascading waterfall that was carefully floodlit to be on view from the dining-room. Cameron's Lamborghini fitted perfectly into its surroundings and the young liveried attendant who drove it away to park it tried, unsuccessfully, to hide his delight at being in charge of such a superbly regal machine.

'You've made his day,' Candy remarked with a smile as they entered the huge, thickly carpeted foyer, the combined smell of expensive perfume and hothouse flowers rich in the scented air.

'Magnanimity is my second name,' Cameron said drily, taking her arm as he led her towards the restaurant, where their coats were whisked away by one waitress as another showed them to their table in a discreet little alcove for two overlooking the beautiful gardens and silently flowing water. 'They open the doors in the summer, weather permitting; I understand it's quite a spectacle,' Cameron remarked as he looked up from his contemplation of the wine list to find her engrossed in the magical picture outside. 'You haven't been here before?'

'Hardly.' She looked at him wryly, her expression candid. 'It's not the usual haunt of the average schoolteacher, is it?'

'I guess not.' He smiled slowly. 'But then the average schoolteacher doesn't have hair like liquid fire and skin like silk.'

'No?' She was mesmerised by the look in his eyes as a slow flicker of excitement shivered down her spine.

'No.' He leant across the table, touching her cheek lightly with the tip of one finger. 'Or the courage and tenacity of a modern day

Boadicea. I used to wonder about that queen of the Iceni when I was younger, attacking the Roman settlements, reducing London to ashes, and then, rather than falling into the hands of her hated enemies, putting an end to her own life by poison. Yes, I used to wonder if such a woman could have existed. But now I know.'

'Don't make me into something I'm not, Cam,' she pleaded quietly.

'I've no need to do that.' He smiled sardonically. 'Believe me, Candy, I have enough trouble coping with what you are than to try and imagine more.'

'Cam —— ' The waitress interrupted her and as she settled back in her seat after giving her order she felt maybe it was as well. She had just been about to reveal how she felt about him and, looking now at his hard, handsome face as he gazed over the small dance-floor to one side of them, she doubted if he had meant his words as they had sounded. He was enormously wealthy, handsome and with a special sort of charisma that would ensure he was never short of female company if he so desired it. She was an ordinary schoolteacher from a small village and her sister had been the means of driving him from his home and country under a cloud as well as being the cause of the final estrangement from his father. She didn't really know him at all; she was only just beginning to understand him a little; but she loved him with all her heart. It was hopeless.

'Why the sad face?' He gestured the wine waiter away and poured the wine he had chosen himself, offering her her glass and watching in evident satisfaction as she relished the taste. 'A couple of glasses of that and you'll pass the evening in a happy daze,' he said teasingly. 'You aren't allowed to drink this stuff with a miserable expression.'

'I don't want to be in a daze, happy or otherwise,' she answered spontaneously with more truth than tact. 'I want to remember every minute of this evening.' His eyes narrowed at her words, but he said nothing, settling back in his seat with that curious waiting expression on his face that always made her feel slightly uncomfortable.

The food was delicious, but she had known it would be, and she relaxed as the meal progressed and they kept to light small talk. She would have to tell him why she had gone to see him today, but that could wait. For the moment it was too intoxicating to be sitting here like this, laughing and talking, to do anything to spoil the mood.

It was as they were having coffee that she raised the subject. Several couples were already dancing and she felt Cameron would ask her once their coffee was finished. She really couldn't face being in his arms until she had spoken, confessed how wrong she had been.

'I suppose you're wondering why I came to see you today?' she said slowly, as they sat watching a particularly small, plump man of well past middle-age whisk a young blonde about the floor as though he were twenty-one.

'His daughter?' Cameron raised laughing, cynical eyebrows as he turned to her and then his expression straightened as her words registered. 'Not particularly.' He looked up at her carefully. 'Should I be?'

'You know I've been away for Easter?' This wasn't going to be easy and he wasn't helping at all, whether by design or accident she wasn't sure.

'No.' Now the old familiar shutter came down, turning the brilliant eyes grey-blue and hardening his classical features into stone. 'I told you; I had guests.'

'I went to see Michelle.' For a moment she wasn't sure if he had heard her. There was no movement in the cold face watching her so intently, no flicker in the piercing eyes.

'And?' It was only one word, but it made Candy shiver.

'And she told me the truth.'

'Which version?' There was a dark anger in the blue eyes and she felt it was directed solely against her, although she didn't understand why.

'The real version.' Her voice was tight now. 'The same thing she told your father all those years ago and my parents after the baby was born.'

'I see.' He settled back in his seat and she saw his mouth was a thin white line. 'And I

thought you came out with me tonight because you'd been thinking about things
yourself, even perhaps beginning to believe
and trust me a little. But you'd been to see
big sister, who'd started you on a guilt trip,
if I'm not mistaken.'

'It's not like that,' she protested faintly,
horrified at his reaction.

'No? Stop fooling yourself, Candy. When
Michelle told you the truth you felt a heavy
dose of remorse about me. I can see it. It's
written in every beautiful, vulnerable line of
your face.' He glared at her angrily. 'I can do
without your pity. There might be a lot of
things I want from you, but, rest assured, pity
sure isn't one of them!'

'Cam, listen; I need to explain —— ' She
stopped, wide-eyed and white-faced, as he
raised an imperious hand, his eyes flashing
blue fire.

'I don't want to discuss it any further tonight, Candy. You're here, whatever your
motive. Let's leave it like that, shall we?'

'No, we won't!' she spat furiously as, in
spite of all her good intentions, her temper

rose to match his. 'Why can't you just stop talking and listen for once?'

'Me stop talking and listen?' He glowered at her, his expression a subtle blend of amazement and fury. 'Well, that's rich, coming from you. Since that first time we met up on the hills you've done nothing but jump to conclusions, most of them blatantly wrong.' The waitress who was coming to replenish their coffee-cups took one look at their faces and disappeared in the opposite direction, her head lowered.

'Really?' She scowled at him angrily. 'And I suppose I imagined those first words you spoke to me, threatening to shoot Jasper? That sure beat any "How nice to meet you" or "How do you do?" I've heard recently. Talk about how to win friends and influence people!'

He had the grace to look slightly discomfited at that, a dull red searing momentarily under his cheekbones. 'You know I wouldn't harm a hair on Jasper's head.'

'I do now,' she retorted quickly. 'But when some bearded stranger leaps out with a loaded gun looking like the wild man of Borneo one tends to do what he says and ask questions later.'

'Oh, for crying out loud.' He ran his hand through his hair in the gesture she was beginning to know so well and it wrung at her heart, dissolving her anger and turning her eyes brilliant with unshed tears. How could she reach him? It was as though there were a high, solid wall round him, and she had to admit quite a few bricks had been put in place by herself.

'Look, Cam,' she began quietly, wanting to reach out and touch his hand, but not quite having the courage. 'I didn't come here tonight because I feel guilty or sorry for you or anything else like that.'

'No?' He looked at her hard. 'You were coming to the house today to apologise for misjudging me, right?'

'Yes,' she admitted carefully.

'And after I'd opened my big mouth and told you a little about my father I can imagine Monica and Michelle added their version too.

Right again?' His eyes didn't leave her face and she couldn't lie.

'Yes, but——'

'That's all I need to know.' She stared at him with a mixture of exasperation and helplessness. She didn't feel pity for him, couldn't he see that? Love, desire, need—these had their places in her heart, but pity? Never. He was mistaking tenderness and compassion for something he found abhorrent. She admired the way he had risen above obstacles that would have crushed a lesser soul, but in doing so he had built a defence that she was beginning to feel was impenetrable.

'Let me make one thing plain, Candy.' All emotion had left his face now and as she stared into his cold blue eyes she knew she had lost. 'Compared to some, my start in life wasn't too bad, and, once grown, we're responsible for our own destiny. Life owes us nothing; it's up for grabs and to cry for the moon just gives one a sore throat.'

'That sounds...hard.' She kept her voice calm and cool.

'Life is hard,' he said soberly.

'And you never cry for the moon?'

'I didn't say I was perfect.' There was that strange expression on his face again and she felt she was missing something vitally important. 'But I'm learning.'

She felt as though she were playing a part in a macabre play for the rest of the evening. They danced, they talked, but Cameron was far from her, holding himself in some sort of iron restraint that was terrifying for the strength of character it revealed.

It was late when they left the hotel, driving home through the quiet, deserted countryside in silence, each lost in their own thoughts. The final cataclysm to the evening began innocently enough, but its shock waves were to stretch into the weeks ahead, distorting whatever they touched.

'Oh, my flower!' As they drew into Candy's drive she clutched the top of her dress in panic. 'I've lost my flower, Cam.' It was the only thing he had ever given her and now it was gone.

'Not to worry.' He seemed quite impervious to her distress, his male mind working on logic. 'It served its purpose for the evening.'

'But I wanted to keep it.' The loss had assumed momentous proportions suddenly. 'Don't you see?' She realised afterwards that she had been asking him more than a surface question about the flower, the strain of the last few weeks spilling over around the orchid.

'Well, it's gone.' He looked at her in the darkness. 'I can always get you another if it means so much.'

'But I want *that* one!' That was the one he had given her at the foot of the stairs with a soft light in his eyes; that was the one he had fixed on her dress with such gentleness. Couldn't he understand?

He shrugged lightly. 'I'll get you a basketful tomorrow.'

'I told you, I don't want another one; it was that one that meant something. Forget it; it's not important.' The look on her face belied her words as she glared at him angrily.

'What on earth have I done now?' he asked softly as a hard glint lit the blue eyes.

'I said forget it.' Her voice was a bark, but he heard the anger only, not recognising the hurt in its brittle depths.

'Forget it?' he said with a harsh laugh. 'I wish I could forget it, Candy, forget this place, forget the ties holding me here, forget you.'

'Well, what's stopping you?' she asked in a voice throbbing with emotion.

'This!' He had moved across her like before, but this time there was no gentle persuasion in his movements, just fierce, cold anger and furious passion. She realised with a feeling of panic that the tight control he had been showing all evening had finally snapped, as he took her lips in a cruel punishment of a kiss, one arm round her waist and the other holding her head against his mouth. She struggled even as she knew the futility of it, his superior weight and strength holding her immobile with effortless ease. The kiss went on and on, hard and searing and vital, and when at last he raised his head to stare down into her dazed, shocked eyes the look on his face frightened her more than the violence of what had gone before.

'Look what you're doing to me.' His face was still so close to hers that she could see the upward curl of his eyelashes above the narrowed eyes filled with self-contempt. 'Do you know I want to take you now, here, even knowing it's against your will and that you hate me? I want to possess you, to make it impossible for you ever to forget me, to be the first. I want you, Candy.' Her name was a long groan and then she was free as he jerked away, opening his door and moving round the car to open her door and almost drag her out into the cold blackness.

As the car screeched down the drive and roared off into the distance she stood completely still, unable to move, her head spinning and a feeling of utter disorientation gripping her mind. What had happened had taken place so quickly she could almost have felt she had imagined it if it weren't for her swollen, bruised lips and aching body. She touched her mouth gingerly with a trembling hand, half expecting to see blood on her fingers. She should be feeling enraged, frightened, but there had been something in his very savagery, his helpless capitulation to his feelings, that had thrilled her even as she had fought him. She shook her head in disgust. What was *she* turning him into? Ha! What was *he* turning her into?

But she loved *him*. She didn't even feel the chill of the night as she stood, swaying slightly, in the darkness. That was why his touch, even in anger, could stir her heart and her body.

And Cameron? Her eyes were bleak as she gazed unseeing up into the black sky alive with millions of tiny, twinkling stars. He wanted her. Simple animal lust. He had told her as much.

'Oh, help me.' She hadn't prayed with such vehemence since she was a child. 'Please help me; I can't bear this.' She didn't know if it was for him or herself that she felt such desolation, such hopelessness, but as she stood in the cold darkness with her face raised to the sky the tears ran down her face in a hot, scalding torrent; but she wasn't even aware she was weeping.

CHAPTER EIGHT

'Hi! I'm home!' Candy called automatically as she entered the house the next evening after her first day at work after the Easter holidays. The day had been a trying one, whether due to the children's exuberance after two weeks of running wild or her own preoccupation with her thoughts she wasn't sure, but, whatever, she had been immensely relieved when the old clock on the wall had chimed the hour. Even Kevin had seemed difficult, getting the same sum wrong over and over again in spite of her having gone through it with him several times, and she had finally snapped at him, much to his chagrin, and earned a furiously disapproving glance from Julie in the process. They had parted friends after a quick cuddle, but the small incident had upset her and added to the ton weight pressing down on her head.

'Mum?' She came to a halt in the doorway to the kitchen to find her mother clasped tightly in her father's arms, her lined face awash with tears, and Jasper sitting in woebegone silence by their side without a wag left in his tail. 'Mum, what is it?'

A helpless wave of the hand was the only answer she received and she turned quickly to her father, her dark eyes anxious. 'Dad?'

'It's OK, it's OK.' Her father gave a dazed smile as he kissed the top of her mother's head. 'It's just that I've taken early retirement; it all happened a bit suddenly today and——'

'Cam's finished you?' Her eyes stretched wider as her father nodded. 'The dirty swine!' She was out of the kitchen like a small whirlwind, the slam of the front door drowning the sound of her father's voice as he called her back. She had used the Mini for work and the keys were still in the ignition— a practice her father highly disapproved of— and she reached thirty mph in the blink of an eye as she roared off, disappearing in a whirl of exhaust fumes as her parents reached the drive.

'You did it. You really did it, Cam,' she muttered disbelievingly as she took a corner almost on two wheels, her tyres yelping a harsh protest. This was her punishment for offending him; he was taking out his spite on two dear people who had shown him only understanding and compassion. 'How could you?' she ground out between clenched teeth, feeling a murderous rage sweeping her body as she hurled into his drive, scattering gravel in a whirling arc as she brought the car to a very professional emergency stop.

Mrs Baines answered the door almost immediately and Candy forced herself to speak politely to the surprised little woman, who took in her flushed face and blazing eyes with a little 'oh' of apprehension.

'Where is he, Mrs Baines?'

'In the study, dear, but I don't think...' Whatever Mrs Baines thought Candy would never know because she was through the hall and outside the door before the small housekeeper could blink. She didn't knock, opening the door with a violence that forced it back at such a speed it almost shut again.

'What the hell...?' Cameron had been working behind his desk, but leapt to his feet at her entrance, his dark face thunderous. 'Have you gone mad?'

'Yes, I've gone mad!' She was aware of Mrs Baines shutting the door behind her and that they were alone, but that wouldn't have made any difference to the furious tirade anyway. 'I went mad the day you came back here and I haven't been sane since.'

'Charming.' He glared at her furiously. 'Am I supposed to know what this latest little witch-hunt is all about?'

'Are you supposed to know?' she shrieked as the last vestige of control slipped. 'You've just got rid of my father, who's worked for your rotten family since he left school, just through sheer spite, and you ask me if you are supposed to know!' He was leaning over one side of his desk and she over the other, their faces inches apart. 'I know Michelle played a filthy trick on you and I've been less than welcoming since you came home, but to sack someone who's given your estate the best years of his life to satisfy some twisted desire for revenge ... it's ... it's immoral.'

'Have you quite finished?' he asked icily as he straightened into a standing position before seating himself once more at the desk.

'Finished? I haven't even started,' she answered wildly, her eyes huge in her white face and her red hair tumbling round her shoulders in glorious disarray. 'You're —— '

'That's enough.' Something in his face, combined with the snarl of a voice, brought her voice to a halt. 'In fact that's more than enough.' He leant back in his chair, his eyes splintered glass and his face stony. 'I presume you haven't discussed this properly with your parents?'

'When I came home from work it was to see Mum crying and Dad trying to comfort her,' she said angrily. 'It doesn't take the Brain of Britain to put two and two together and reach four.'

'Or, in this case, five.' The first deadly trickle of doubt crept down her spine.

'Five?'

'I stand corrected. Nine or ten.' He rose now and moved round the desk towards her and it took all the will-power she possessed not to back away. She had never seen such undiluted fury before; it was almost tangible. 'What's this?' He picked up an official-looking document from the desk and thrust it into her nerveless fingers. 'Read it.'

She stared at the paper, but the black figures danced and waved in front of her eyes and she looked up helplessly. 'I can't.'

'You damn well will! Sit down and look at it.' He pushed her into the seat facing the desk and walked back to his own, sitting down without another word and waiting silently while she read. It was like her own epitaph, a fitting memorial to all her doubts and mistrust.

'You've given them the house?' She looked up in a daze.

'And a pension for life at the same rate as your father's salary. Combined with his own pension, that should enable them to live very nicely and do some of the things they've always wanted to. I take it you didn't wait to find all this out?' She shook her head vacantly. 'Well, why should you?' His voice was dripping venom. 'There is nothing, absolutely nothing you think me incapable of. "Sacking" your father would almost rate as one of my finer deeds, would it not?'

'Cameron —— '

'I care for your father, Candy, believe it or not. I wanted him to have some time with Vivien, free of financial pressure, while they were both still young enough to enjoy it. You think I won't miss him? He knows this place and all its warts and pimples like the back of his hand. It will be impossible to replace him. And I shall miss *him*, his genuine, unaffected friendship and desire to smooth my path.'

'Cam —— '

'Get out, Candy.' It was a stranger in front of her and she stared at him, horrified, as he faced her, his eyes as cold as ice and his mouth a thin line in the stark whiteness of his face.

'Please, Cam —— '

'Please, Cam?' He repeated her words in biting mockery. 'That's what Michelle said that night ten years ago. "Please, Cam, please." I've heard of lightning striking twice...' He stopped suddenly. 'Get out, Candy, get out before I do something I will regret for the rest of my life.'

She moved slowly, like an old, old woman, stumbling as she made for the door, but he made no move to help her. His countenance could have been set in stone for all the emotion he showed. She tried once more as she reached the doorway, turning in an effort to reach him, but the passionate words in her heart died on her lips as she saw his eyes. They were deadly, full of cold savagery and a kind of bitter contempt that pierced her through. And it was all her fault! Her tears blinded her as she left the house, and she reached the sanctuary of her little faithful Mini with something akin to hysteria sweeping over her body. How could she have been so foolish? To destroy even the little they had in one fell swoop!

The next few days felt like years. Life was reduced to existence and she became little more than an automaton as she went about her daily tasks, a vacant, self-acting machine merely simulating flesh and blood.

Her parents had been discretion itself when she had returned home after her abortive visit to Cameron, their anxious faces reaching out to her in spite of her misery. 'Don't worry, it's OK,' she had said quietly, a blessed numbness taking over her mind. 'Cam explained about the pension and so on.'

'Before you had your say or after?' her father asked perceptively.

'After.' She looked at them with blank eyes.

'Oh, Candy.' Her mother sighed softly. 'We tried to stop you, but you'd already gone. I can see how it must have looked to you, but I was so overcome with his generosity; it's a dream come true. They were tears of joy, do you see?'

'Yes, I see.' She threw a despairing glance at her father. 'Well, you always said my temper would cause me to catch my toe one day, Dad. In this case I think it was the whole foot.'

'That bad?' her father asked softly.

'You'd better believe it.' She tried a weak smile and made for the stairs. 'Bed, I think. Tomorrow is a new day, or so they say.' And it had been, dismal and joyless and bleak like the ones that followed.

'Sue's on the phone, Candy.' She gave a sigh of relief as she left the self-imposed task of weeding the flower-beds, pulling off her gardening gloves as she walked towards the house. The last few days had been bad enough, caught as she was in an empty void that seemed to stretch on and on, but she had been dreading the weekend without even the children to distract her from her morbid, inward-looking thoughts.

'Candy, baby!' Sue's cheerful voice rattled down the line. 'Doing anything tonight?'

'Not that I know of,' Candy answered slowly. She liked Sue; she always had. Her old schoolfriend was totally without guile and as open as the day was long. An evening in her company was always uncomplicated and easy, which was just what she needed at the moment.

'The gang's meeting at the Cross Keys at eight,' Sue said brightly. 'See you there?'

'Maybe.' She would have preferred it with just Sue, but Saturday night was Saturday night.

'Not "maybe",' Sue returned firmly. 'Everyone's saying they haven't seen you in weeks, Candy; what gives?'

'I've just been busy.' There was no way she was discussing Cameron with anyone.

'Too busy.' Sue's voice took on a note of concern. 'You looked awful when I saw you in the post office the other day. Come out for a drink, Candy; you needn't stay all night. Say yes, go on.'

'OK.' She hadn't the interest or the energy to argue, and besides, the thought of another night with her mind performing a relentless post-mortem on her last conversation with Cameron was anything but appealing.

'Great, see you at eight, then.'

It took her exactly five minutes to get ready later that day, merely changing one pair of jeans for another and pulling a fresh sweater over her head after she had washed her hands and scrubbed her nails free of garden dirt. She looped her hair into a quick pony-tail without even glancing in the mirror and, picking up her bag from the chair, called goodbye to her parents as she walked downstairs. 'See you later, won't be late.' They had been immersed in travel brochures and had found it hard to even look up as she paused by the lounge door. Only Jasper was pleased to see her, giving her a wag of his tail as he lay stretched out in front of the roaring coal fire in doggy bliss, toasting first one side and then the other with a silly grin on his face.

It was only a five-minute walk to the Cross Keys and the attractive little pub, with its white-washed, ivy-clad stone walls and beautifully thatched roof was full to bursting when she entered the low, arched door nearly an hour late.

'Candy!' Immediately Sue was by her side and she saw most of their friends were grouped round the huge old wooden fireplace on carved wooden benches either side of the crackling log fire. 'I've got you a drink in; come and sit down.' She hesitated slightly as she noticed David was in the party and then followed Sue over, hiding her annoyance as David made a great show of providing a space next to him. They had only met once, by chance, since that night at his house, followed by a telephone call by him the next day when she had made it very plain she considered their somewhat tenuous friendship well and truly over. He had been first indignant and then abrasively rude and the parting had been a sour one. Now, however, he seemed all smiles and jollity, his good-looking, weak face glowing, and not just with the heat of the fire, she suspected.

'What have you been doing with yourself, Candy?' one of the others asked genially. 'We've missed you.'

'Oh, this and that.' Candy smiled dismissively, but then her expression froze as David's voice sounded innocently by her side.

'Maybe you ought to ask *who* she's been doing it with.' His tone was jocular and she suspected no one else caught the thread of maliciousness.

'What's this? A mystery?' Sue took up the remark laughingly, her good-natured face merry. 'I love a good mystery.'

'No mystery, Sue.' Now one or two of the others sensed the barbed content of David's words and she noticed his voice was slightly slurred. She was right; he had been drinking too much. He never had been able to hold his liquor. 'Our little Candy has got herself a suitor; isn't that right, lovely?' He smiled at her with his mouth as his eyes flashed bitterly over her face. 'Flying high, aren't we?'

'I don't think Candy wants to discuss this any further, David.' Martin, the doctor's son, spoke firmly and cuttingly, and David immediately subsided into hurt silence, sensing the united disapproval of those present as Candy's face turned a bright shade of red.

'Only having a joke...' he mumbled to no one in particular, earning a measured glance of disgust from Sue in the process. 'My round, eh?' By the time he returned with the tray of drinks the atmosphere had cleared and after the pointed rebuff by Martin he had obviously decided to behave himself, joining in the general conversation carefully. If he was sitting a little too close to Candy she decided to ignore it to avoid a scene, although the feel of his soft, warm thigh next to hers was making her feel a little sick. And to think she had once counted this creep as one of her friends!

She was aware of the door behind her opening and shutting a number of times and then, to her annoyance, she felt David's arm snake along the back of the bench behind her to rest in line with her shoulders, his hand hanging over her arm. Damn, damn, damn. She needed this aggravation like a hole in the head! She glanced at him carefully to find him smiling at her with a strange gleam in his pale eyes. 'Anything wrong?' he murmured softly, and she forced a cool smile to her lips as she shook her head slowly. There was no way he was going to engineer a scene here in front of everyone. If that was his little game she could stick this farce for another hour or so and then make a quick getaway. There was little he could do in front of all the others.

'My round, I think?' She stood up gratefully after a few minutes, thankful to get the feel of him off her flesh, but he stood up quickly too, his face smiling.

'I'll help you.' It would have been churlish to refuse and she could escape in a while anyway, so she nodded curtly and made her way to the bar, conscious of him a step behind her. As she gave the order to the barman David slid his arms either side of her waist so she was pinned between the counter and his body in what looked, to anyone watching, like an intimate embrace.

'David, I've just about had enough of this,' she hissed quietly, turning at an angle to look into his face.

'Of what?' He was grinning inanely and she would have given the world to slap the silliness out of his face.

'Of you mauling me about,' she murmured angrily. 'Any more and I don't care about the others, so help me. I'll hit you where you stand!'

'Nownonow.' The drink was telling and his words were slurring together unintelligibly.

'Why be l' this? I thought we were friends? Can't w' be friends?'

'If you want to be friends get your arms off me,' she said quietly. 'I mean it, David, now!'

'Jus' one littl' kiss, then. Jus' for ole times' sake, and then Davey will be a good boy.' She glanced at him in exasperation. There was no way he was going to move until she gave him a peck. She could tell that note of belligerence in his voice meant the drink was giving him Dutch courage, but, false or not, he meant to prove his point.

'Just one, then, and that's it.' She moved round to kiss his cheek, but, with a dexterity that made her suspect he wasn't as drunk as he seemed, he brought his arms up to hold her to him in a great bear-hug at the same time as his moist lips clamped on her mouth. She was too surprised at his audacity to react for a moment and then, as hot rage flooded her stiff body, she went to lash out, only to find herself free and a cool, indolent voice speaking to one side of her head.

'Good evening, Candy. I trust you are enjoying yourself?' She turned to find

Cameron's hard, cold eyes a few inches from hers, Monica and Bill's unhappy faces in the background.

'Cam...' The shock of seeing him again momentarily robbed her of speech and then she was conscious of him nodding to David, his eyes icy.

'Hello again. David, isn't it?'

'Yeh, that's right.' David sounded immensely pleased with himself and now Candy knew why. He had obviously noticed Cameron come in some time ago and had planned this little charade for his benefit!

Cameron's next words confirmed her suspicions. 'We're just off, only called in for a quick one.' He nodded to them both distantly. 'See you around, then.'

'Seems as if it's hello and goodbye.' Monica had moved to Cameron's side and as she took Candy's arm Cameron was forced to wait for her. 'We must meet up again soon.'

'I'd like that,' Candy answered weakly as the barman's voice sounded in her ear.

'Eleven pounds twenty, miss.'

'I'll get it.' David jumped in before she had time to open her mouth. 'Can't have my girl paying for the drinks, can we?' His voice was perfectly clear and distinct now, and as she went to argue Monica tapped her lightly on the shoulder.

'Bye, then, Candy, I'll be in touch.' The three of them turned away in one movement and she was left with David and the tray of drinks and a great void where her stomach should have been. As she watched Cameron's dark head disappear out of the door she wanted to cry and scream and shout and throw things, but instead she turned back to David with a bitter, cold smile twisting her mouth.

'Well done, David.' He looked slightly startled at the direct assault, but said nothing. 'What have I ever done to you to deserve this?'

'All's fair in love and war, sweetheart,' he said brightly, his light blue eyes with their pale lashes resembling those of a mindless goldfish in a bowl. 'I did see you first, remember?'

'David, I wouldn't have you gift-wrapped,' she said cuttingly, leaving him at the bar as she walked over to the others and collected her coat and bag. 'David's bringing the drinks and I'm off,' she said quietly to Sue.

'Everything all right?' Sue followed her to the doorway, her eyes dark with concern.

'Far from it, but I'll give you a ring and explain things,' Candy said tightly. 'Suffice to say if I have to stay here one more minute in the company of that gormless moron there'll be murder done.'

'Right.' Sue took a step backwards at the savagery in Candy's voice. 'Right, then.'

There was no sign of Cameron outside, but then she had known there wouldn't be. He would be long since gone, no doubt thinking she was wrapped in David's arms and enjoying his company just like maybe her sister would have been? She clasped her arms tightly round her waist and groaned out loud. There was no way she could reach him now, nothing she could do. The die had been cast ten years ago and all the love in the world couldn't change things now.

She walked home slowly, blind to the
mellow charm and serene beauty around her,
passing the tiny church with its pencil-slim
spire with unseeing eyes. She had lost, completely and irrevocably, and now the only path
left open to her was to leave the village and
all its inhabitants as quickly as she could.

CHAPTER NINE

CANDY could never remember much about the following two weeks, but on May the first, with new life bursting out around her, vibrant and pulsating in the new leaves on the trees and tiny budding flowers, she suddenly came to herself. What was she doing? What *was* she doing? This wasn't like her, to give in miserably, to accept defeat, to creep away into a hole and die. She had always known exactly what she wanted out of life and she still did, except that now it had all changed. Now it began and ended with a tall dark man who had eyes the colour of blue ice and a heart to match.

Monica hadn't contacted her, but that didn't surprise her. She had seen something change in the warmth of the older woman's eyes when David had spoken, insinuating she was 'his girl'. If she wanted to speak to Monica she realised she would have to make

248

the first move and she had the feeling she would desperately need an ally in the enemy camp before she was through.

She rang Monica at lunchtime the next day and, as she had expected, there was a definite element of reserve in the other woman's voice. 'Candy, this is a nice surprise.' Candy smiled to herself grimly. From the cool note in Monica's voice she gathered the solicitor was not one for hiding her feelings.

'I don't suppose it is, really.' There was a blank silence at the other end of the phone and then Monica spoke again, her voice fractionally warmer.

'Well, a surprise, anyway. I must confess I didn't expect to hear from you again after the other night. I gather that young man is your boyfriend?'

'No, he is not,' Candy said vehemently. 'He's the biggest creep this side of the sun and quite loathsome.'

The silence was a little longer this time. 'Do I take it you've fallen out?' Monica asked coolly.

'Monica, we were never "in",' Candy said sharply. 'The whole thing was contrived by David for Cameron's benefit. Some sort of pathetic "hands off" idea, I think.'

'It's worked.'

Candy bit on her lip anxiously. This was going to be harder than she had thought. 'Let me make one thing clear, Monica. I have never been out with David in that way, whatever impression he likes to give, and if he was the last man on this earth I would still run a mile. Is that plain enough?'

'It's not me you want to convince, is it?' There was a long pause and then Monica spoke again. 'I'm sorry, Candy, but I have to say I don't understand you, I really don't.' That makes two of us, Candy thought grimly. 'I'm not sure if you want to have your cake and eat it, but if you do I can assure you it won't work, not with Cam.'

'I know that and nothing is further from my mind,' Candy said quickly. 'Please, Monica, I need your help.'

'I can't help you, Candy.' There was a great depth of weariness in Monica's voice. 'He's going to Australia and that's that. Nothing will change his mind now.'

'He's doing what?' Candy almost dropped the phone in her shock.

'He's going to Australia,' Monica repeated in surprise. 'Didn't you know? I thought that's why you'd rung. I'd have thought you'd be clapping your hands with joy; it's what you've angled for all along, isn't it?'

'Yes...no...well, at first I wanted him to leave,' Candy stammered miserably. 'But that was before...' Her voice trailed away. 'Why is he going, Monica?' she asked in a small, flat voice.

'Candy, you are enough of a woman to know the answer to that one, especially after that night in the pub,' Monica answered firmly. 'The estate is up for sale and most of his business interests in this country are being wound up. He means it, child; he isn't fooling.'

'I see.' She could hear the sound of another phone ringing in the background and men's voices rising and falling in some sort of discussion. 'I'm sorry, Monica; you're obviously very busy. I'll call back some other time.'

'OK.' There was a pause. 'Candy?'

'Yes.'

'Oh, nothing. I've said enough. Keep in touch.' As the phone was replaced at the other end Candy stood in frozen immobility, her mind reeling. What had Monica meant about her being enough of a woman to know why he was leaving? She couldn't have meant... Her heart began to pound so hard that she felt quite ill. How did a man like him show love? Even his acts of compassion and understanding were done silently; she would never have found out about his kindness to Kevin and his mother if Monica hadn't told her. And now her parents. Oh, Cam...

He wanted her; she knew that much. Even if he hadn't admitted it the other night she knew beyond doubt that her body held physical attraction for him. Right from the first it had been there in his eyes, his every expression, but love...? Men could separate love and desire into neat compartments, unlike most women. Especially a man like him, experienced and worldly wise with a fierce sense of independence that had been cultivated since childhood to compensate for a lifetime of crippling, arid loneliness.

Her mind jolted at the last thought. He had no one; he never really had anyone. How could she *not* tell him how she felt? This faint, tentative hope she had might be wrong—it might just be plain, physical attraction he felt for her—but with this man, this precious man, there was no room for false pride. She had to make him understand she loved him and then, if he had nothing to give her in return, leave as his friend. But he might, he just might, feel something for her? The wild surge of painful joy swept over her in an overwhelming flood before she dampened it down. Don't, don't think of it now, she told herself firmly. Just do what you've got to do.

The afternoon crawled by, but eventually the clock ticked the last minute away and she emptied the school in record time, locking the heavy old door behind her with a feeling of panic gripping her throat until she could hardly breathe. This was madness, complete and utter madness, a crazy gamble that was going to leave her looking the biggest fool on earth! And the alternative? her mind asked her logically. A lifetime of regret, of not knowing, of bitter anger that she hadn't had the courage to follow a dream.

'Mrs Baines?' As she stood at the top of the wide, sweeping steps she saw the little housekeeper's customary smile was missing, and that convinced her like nothing else that this nightmare was a reality. 'Can I have a word with Cam, please?'

'I don't know if he'll see you.' Mrs Baines looked at her sadly. 'He left word he wasn't to be disturbed. He's been working all hours trying to get everything to rights before he leaves.'

'He's going soon?' Candy whispered softly.

'In three days, dear. I don't know, what a to-do.' Mrs Baines shook her head despondently. 'And here was me thinking I'd be here for life. Not that he hasn't been generous— oh, no, more than generous—but I want to stay here. You know what I mean, dear?'

'Yes, I know.' Candy looked towards the closed study door. 'Could you just see...?'

'Come on in and sit down a minute,' Mrs Baines said, quietly opening the front door wide and gesturing to the drawing-room. 'I'll try, but I'm not promising anything, mind. Funny mood he's been in for days.' She was back within minutes, her face apologetic. 'No luck, I'm afraid. Can I take a message? He definitely won't see you, Miss Candy.'

'Mrs Baines, it's essential I see him,' Candy said urgently. 'Let me go in, please.'

'I can't do that —— '

'I'll take all the blame, I promise. I'll say I barged past you or something, but I have to see him, I just have to. Please, Mrs Baines.'

'Oh, I don't know.' Mrs Baines shook her head in confusion. 'I'm too old for these sorts of goings-on. Mr Charles would turn in his grave.' She looked at Candy's pleading face and shook her head again. 'Go on with you, then. But don't outstay your welcome, mind.'

Welcome? What welcome? Candy thought wryly as she walked swiftly out of the room. She knocked once on the door and then opened it gingerly, stepping inside as her stomach lurched alarmingly. He was sitting at his desk, his elbows on the gleaming dark wood and his head in his hands.

'Has she gone, Mrs Baines?'

She tried to speak, but her mind had gone blank with the thrill of seeing him again. The dark, shining hair, his big, broad shoulders, hunched now and curiously defenceless. And he had been going to leave without a word and she would never have seen him again. Oh, Cameron.

'I said...' As he raised his head and saw her standing there he rose so quickly that the chair shot out from under his legs to ricochet against the wall and skid halfway across the room. In that second of stark surprise his face was naked and she saw something that gave her the strength to continue.

'I had to come, Cam. Please listen to me.' At the sound of her voice the mask settled instantly over his face, clothing his features with cold remoteness.

'There's something wrong?' he asked harshly, but she noticed the hand that raked back his hair was shaking slightly. You do care, Cam, she prayed silently; I know you do.

'I've been wrong; you're wrong now.' She took a deep breath and spoke straight from the heart. 'I didn't understand when you first came back, Cam, I was too tied up with things in the past to see the truth, even though it was staring me right in the face. I knew you affected me, but I wouldn't let myself probe any deeper than that. I pretended it was just a physical thing between us.'

'Pretended?' His voice was cruel.

'Yes, pretended!' She took a step towards him, but he gave her such a glance of withering scorn that she stopped uncertainly. 'Look, I know how it looked with David the other night, but that was just him being ... being——'

'Being protective of his property?' He was being deliberately insulting, but she quenched the spurt of anger his cold insolence awoke with iron determination. If she lost her temper now it was the end, really the end.

'Being pathetic.' She looked at him hard. 'He thought it would get to you even though he knew by then there was no hope of my ever going out with him.'

'And why should he think that?' He eyed her coldly.

'Because he feels you like me and he knows...' she paused for the fraction of a second '...he knows I love you.'

'You expect me to believe that?' She could have believed there was liquid ice flowing in his veins from the chill that was emanating from him, but she *had* seen something in his face before he had recovered himself sufficiently to don the mask. It had been fierce hunger, blazing need and some other element she dared not put a name to.

'Yes, I do.' She looked him full in the face. 'You should know one thing about me by now: I do speak the truth.'

'And why have you decided to..."speak the truth" at this moment in time?' he asked flatly. 'What little birdie has been whispering in your ear?'

She took another step towards him and then gestured at the chair in front of her facing the desk. 'Can I sit down a minute?'

'There's no point,' he said evenly as his eyes glittered like blue glass. 'You're leaving in a moment. Now, why this amazing declaration and why now?'

'Because you're going back to Australia in three days' time,' she said quietly.

'Now we're beginning to get somewhere.' He folded his arms and leant back against the wall. 'I suspect that's the first honest thing you've said since you came. What have you done with Mrs Baines, by the way? Tied her to a chair?'

'Don't be ridiculous.' She knew he was trying to provoke her into losing her temper, but she was determined not to bite. 'And I've meant every word I've said, Cam.'

'Have you?' The pose he had taken up was casual enough, but she could feel his body was as tight as a coiled spring. 'I'm sorry, Candy, but that's too big a pill to swallow. You've found out I'm leaving and persuaded yourself it's something to do with you, that you are somehow responsible. Is that approaching the truth?'

Her eyes flickered under his steel gaze. It was the truth, but not the whole story, and certainly not the way he was representing it. 'Partly, but——'

'I thought so.' He laughed harshly. 'Hasn't anyone told you that blood sacrifices finished nearly two thousand years ago? What do you think you're offering me, a nice, friendly affair? Holding hands in the moonlight and a chaste kiss on the cheek? I'd want more, much more; you have no idea——'

'I'm not a child, Cam.' She glared at him as hot colour rose in her cheeks. 'I know——'

'You know nothing, absolutely nothing.' He raked back his hair again and this time his hand was rock-steady. 'You aren't built for casual affairs, Candy. Some women can handle it, but not you. After the first time I'd taken your body you'd feel regret and a sense of betrayal. The next time disgust would begin to emerge. Oh, I'm not saying you'd dislike the physical sensations,' he added quickly as she opened her mouth to speak. 'In fact, I can guarantee that side would be pleasurable for both of us.' A fire blazed to life behind his eyes for a second and then was quenched ruthlessly. 'But soon, after a few weeks, a few months, you'd hate me. The sense of guilt you feel now would be replaced by loathing and self-disgust. I don't want that, Candy. I've done a lot of things in my life I'm not particularly proud of, but I've never knowingly wrecked someone else's.'

'It wouldn't be like that.' She held out her hands in a pleading gesture, her eyes liquid. 'I've told you, I love you——'

'What you feel for me is pity mixed with a heavy dose of misplaced guilt and sexual attraction,' he said coldly. 'The first two I don't need and the latter would be an encumbrance I would find cloying after a time.' He was being deliberately cruel, she knew it, but it still hurt unbearably. 'If I want my physical needs satisfying I prefer to do the choosing at a time to suit me. Have I made myself clear?' She stared at him dumbly with huge brown eyes. 'And the women I would choose are experienced coquettes who can please me as much as I do them. I don't need you round my neck like a millstone, Candy, and that's the end of this conversation.'

He turned away so his back was towards her, leaning both hands against the window-sill, his body taut and still. 'Goodbye, Candy.' She stood for a long moment, too shocked to cry, and then his voice came as a bark. 'I said goodbye, Candy.'

She backed to the door, her hand to her mouth, and then wrenched it open with nerveless fingers, racing across the hall and fumbling with the front door as a stream of hot tears blinded her. She heard the study door bang behind her and froze for a moment, but there were no footsteps coming towards her, no tall dark figure standing watching her.

'Miss Candy? Are you all right?' As she finally tugged the door open Mrs Baines appeared from the drawing-room, her round, plump face lined with concern as she saw Candy's wet, hot cheeks. 'What on earth happened?'

'Nothing, it's nothing...' Candy gasped as she stepped outside into the warm, mellow sunlight of the May evening. Nothing! She had just lost the one thing she wanted in all the world and she called it 'nothing'!

'Is it Mr Cameron? He's upset you?' Mrs Baines followed her out on to the top of the steps, her cheeks shaking with indignation. 'Well, I won't have this. Young master or not, I shall tell him!'

'Please, Mrs Baines.' Candy fought to control herself, her chest heaving with the effort. 'It's not Cam. I've just had a shock.'

'Well, I don't know.' Mrs Baines took a step closer to her, her bright small black eyes anxious. 'If you say so, Miss Candy, but I'm worried about him, I really am. He's not eating and I know he doesn't go to bed till three or four in the morning and then he's up again at six. He can't go on like this; the weight is just dropping off him.'

'Is it?' Candy scrubbed at her face with her handkerchief and blew her nose loudly.

'He walks those poor dogs until their legs are nearly dropping off and comes back with a face like thunder and a temper to match. I tell you, Miss Candy, no one knows what I've had to suffer the last two weeks.'

'Two weeks?' Candy seized on the little woman's words like a terrier with a bone. 'Did you say he's been like this for two weeks?'

'That's right,' said Mrs Baines confidingly. 'You ought to see the meals I've cooked to tempt him, Miss Candy—works of art they are—but no, back they come, untouched.'

'Mrs Baines, I've got to go.' She backed away from the small housekeeper, who was now in full gossip mode. 'I've just remembered an appointment, I'm sorry...'

'All right, dear, all right.' Mrs Baines looked slightly affronted as Candy took off at a gallop across the lawns, reaching the curve of the drive in seconds and leaning back against the gnarled trunk of an old oak tree once she was hidden from the house.

Two weeks. Two weeks! She wanted to dance and shout and then checked herself suddenly. It might not mean anything. It could be something quite different from seeing her with David that had caused this torment, some business pressure that she knew nothing about. She shook her head, her eyes shining. No, she wouldn't believe that. It had to be because he loved her; it had to! He had thought today he was protecting her from herself, that was it.

On the walk home cold, bleak reality set in. Whether he loved her or not he was never going to admit it while he believed what he did. Three days. How could she perform little less than a miracle in three days?

It was in the middle of the night that the idea came to her. She sat bolt upright in bed, unsure whether she had been asleep and dreaming or awake and thinking, but, whatever, she knew what she had to do now. It was going to take some organising and she had less than three days to pull it off, but pull it off she must.

The rest of the night was spent making lists, writing letters and sorting clothes, and when her mother came downstairs at seven the next morning it was to find Candy in the midst of a pile of papers, triumphantly holding her passport aloft. 'Found it!' She gave Vivien a beaming smile. 'I'm going to Australia in two days.'

By nine o'clock she had both given in her notice and arranged a supply teacher for the school as well as having packed one suitcase. At ten she phoned Monica.

'I need to know exactly when and where Cam's flying to Australia from,' she stated with no preliminaries as Monica's voice came warily on the line.

'You do?' Monica hesitated. 'Can I ask why?'

'If you promise to keep it to yourself.'

'Will it hurt Cam if I say yes?'

'I can only say I believe it will hurt him a lot more if you say no,' Candy answered quietly with her fingers crossed.

'I promise.' She thought she detected a hopeful note in Monica's voice.

'I'm going to catch the same flight; it's the only way I can convince him I really do love him and I'm serious, but even then I might fail.'

There was a long, pregnant pause and then, 'Good for you, girl!' Monica had obviously made a decision and was going for it. 'Get a pen and notebook ready; there's a few other things you'll need to see to besides a ticket. You'll need a visa, for one thing. Ready?'

At the end of the conversation Candy's head was reeling and a few pages of the notebook were full of her scribbles. She blessed Monica's efficiency. Every eventuality on the mechanics was covered. If only the emotional side were as simple!

'Candy?' It was the old Monica now, warm and approving. 'Don't take no for an answer. He needs you, desperately.'

'I'll try, but you know Cam,' Candy answered quietly.

'Exactly.'

The next day she went to London to get a visa. She didn't sleep at all that night, except for an hour or so due to total exhaustion in the early morning. She couldn't have explained how she felt to anyone. Her head was throbbing, her stomach was a law unto itself, and nervous excitement had the adrenalin pumping so vigorously through her body that she felt positively hyperactive. If this failed she had lost everything—her job, her savings, but, most importantly, the chance to ever have children and share her life with one man. Because one thing was for sure; if she couldn't have Cameron then she wouldn't have anyone.

She cried once when she said goodbye to Jasper, the feel of his warm, loving body snuggling into her arms and his big square head resting adoringly on her sleeve causing a momentary loss of control. But then the will-power that was an integral part of her make-up came to her aid and she blinked the weakness away, sniffing loudly. She didn't know when she would see him again and he wasn't a young dog... She forced her mind away from depressing thoughts.

Her father had wanted to drive her to the airport, but she had insisted on a taxi, wanting to say goodbye to her parents in their own home and leave them together in familiar sur-roundings when she left. They were still stunned by the suddenness of her decision, but had made no move to dissuade her from her decision, for which she was grateful. It wouldn't have made any difference if they had, but it was good to know she had their support, if not their full understanding.

As the taxi drove her away she looked back through the window one last time to see them hugging each other close, her mother's face awash with tears. It hadn't helped that she couldn't be specific on how long she was going to be away, talking vaguely of weeks or possibly months. She felt they knew, like her, that, whatever the outcome of this endeavour, she could never come back and have things the way they were. If Cameron didn't want her, if she had been hideously wrong, then it would mean a new life somewhere else. There were too many memories tied up in these familiar surroundings.

The airport was a hive of activity when she finally wheeled her loaded trolley into the terminal. She was three hours early, having been gripped by a fear that something would go wrong at the last minute, but it didn't matter. She could wait. Eventually her luggage was checked in, she passed through Customs, and then she was in the departure lounge—and still no Cameron.

She picked up a magazine and flicked idly through the glossy pages. Perhaps she was wrong? Perhaps one of these girls with hair the colour of ripe corn and an hourglass figure would suit him better, all long legs, beautiful clothes and practised seduction? Or how about this one, a sultry brunette with come-to-bed eyes? Or ——

'I don't believe it.' She looked up into a pair of blazing blue eyes as hard as liquid steel. 'I really don't believe it.'

'Hello, Cameron.' He sat down beside her on the cushioned seat, abruptly pushing the magazines into a discarded heap on the floor, his face as black as thunder and his breathing harsh.

'Candy!' He shook his head and took a deep breath, starting again in a more moderate tone. 'What are you doing here, Candy?'

'I'd have thought it was obvious.' She looked at him carefully. He smelt delicious and looked even better, but there were marked

lines of strain round his mouth and eyes, and
Mrs Baines was right: he had lost weight.

He ran a hand over his eyes and leant back
in the seat with a small sigh. 'Indulge me.'

'I'm going to Australia,' she said brightly.

'You're what?' Several passengers sitting
near by cast interested glances in their direction and he moved a little nearer to her,
taking another deep, calming breath.

'You are not.'

'You can't stop me.' She looked him full in
the face. 'I'm twenty-two, Cameron. I can go
where I like.'

'Twenty-two...' He groaned slightly and
shook his head. 'I know how old you are,
Candy; if anyone knows, I do! It's a lot different from thirty-four.'

'Twelve years, to be exact,' she said, still
in the bright voice. 'I'm a schoolteacher; I
know about these things.'

'You know about these things,' he repeated
slowly. 'Carrot-tops, you don't know a thing.
The real world out there would eat you alive.'

'Not with you to look after me.' He froze,
but she went on determinedly, her eyes tight

on his still face. 'I love you, Cam; I always have, but I never knew it. I hated it when you went all those years ago and I hated you for leaving me. Not Michelle, me. Probably if you'd married her my puppy love would have died—it would have had to. But you didn't marry her and then you came back. I'd been fed lies and I believed them at first, but mainly to protect myself from something I couldn't face: that it wasn't what you were supposed to have done to Michelle that hurt so much, but that you left me without a word. You never even said goodbye.'

'Candy——'

'No! You always interrupt me, but not this time, Cam. I'm going to have to have my say this time.' He sank back into his seat, lowering the hand he had raised in protest. 'At first you seemed to do everything to confirm all my worst fears, but even then I couldn't let it alone. If you *had* got Michelle pregnant and left her, if you *had* thrown Kevin and his mother out and sacked Dad...even if all that were true I would still love you. Not respect you as I do, but I'd still love you. You couldn't do anything to kill that.'

'You don't know what you're saying.' The colour had drained from his face, leaving it as white as a sheet, but there was a look in his eyes that caused her heart to leap.

'I do.' There was a thread of the old antagonism in her voice. 'I'll follow you wherever you go, Cam, if that's what it takes to convince you I love you. Until you can tell me, looking me straight in the face, that there is no chance at all for us, that you just don't care for me in that way, I'll carry on following you. I've got no pride where you're concerned, Cam, just love.'

'This is madness, Candy,' he said painfully. 'The village—you can't leave the village and all the children; you know you can't. And you're so young. You can't throw your life away on a whim.'

'I've already given in my notice at work.' She put her hand on his arm, feeling his body tense at her touch. 'And this is no whim. As for being young, I suppose I am in some ways, but there are others where it will take you years to catch up with me. Learning to trust, to be part of a real family, catching up on all the things you've missed out on. And Cam——' she paused as his eyes darkened '—I'm not talking out of pity. You misunderstood the other day and you're doing it again. I love you with all my heart and part of that love wants to make up for all the hurt. Can't you understand that?'

'I dare not understand it.' The words were pulled out of him.

'Cam, I want to be with you wherever you are. Your country will be my country and your friends my friends. I want your children, to see them grow with two parents who love them and each other, to——'

'Don't.' He pulled her to him so violently that her head snapped back on her shoulders. 'We've got to get out of here. I can't talk to you in here.'

'We can't.' She looked at him in amazement. 'The plane is leaving soon; all our luggage——'

'Let it go; I don't care. Let the whole world go.' He had pulled her to her feet and she was following him now at a trot, out through the door into the red tape of officialdom that took long minutes to clear and then through the huge glass doors into the spring sunshine. 'My car's still here; I'd arranged for someone to collect it,' he said dazedly, looking down at her with a look of wonder in his eyes. 'Come on.'

As they drove out of the airport she was aware his body was rigid and his face tense, but there was a growing conviction in her mind that she had won. He might not love her as she loved him, but she could be patient, and it was enough for now that he had listened to her, that he was beginning to trust her a little. She wished he would kiss her, touch her, do anything to reassure the hope in her heart.

Some miles from the airport he swung the car off the road and through a convenient gateway marked 'private', drawing to a halt in a freshly ploughed field. 'Cam?' She looked at him quickly. 'We shouldn't be here; the farmer —— '

'Stop talking,' he said gruffly, resting both hands on the steering-wheel before turning abruptly to face her, his eyes narrowed and his face filled with such raw emotion that she felt suddenly shy. 'Have you any idea, any idea at all how often I've dreamed of something like this over the last few months?'

'You don't have to say that to be kind.' She touched his tanned cheek with the palm of her hand gently, and he gave a deep shudder as her fingers caressed a slow path to his mouth.

'Kind?' His eyes opened wide with amazement as he caught her hand in his, his face strained. 'Who the hell is being kind? You've turned my world upside-down, reduced me to a quivering wreck of my former self, and you think I'd be kind to you?' There was black humour in the dry words, but she looked at him anxiously, her eyes wide.

'You don't hate me?'

'Hate you?' he said hoarsely. He shook his head and placed her hand in her lap firmly, stopping her when she made to take his hand again. 'Listen to me for a minute and don't touch me. You're playing with fire, Candy, and my control is at zero. OK?' She nodded slowly. 'I've never loved anyone before and I'm finding it terrifying; that's the truth.' He cast a wry glance at her flushed face. 'You've got all the power of the world in those tiny hands and I can't do anything about it.' He shook his head again, an almost comical expression of bewilderment softening the harsh features.

'From the first moment I saw you again I wanted you. I didn't know who you were, but I wanted you so badly. There you were, a little slip of a thing in a duffel coat and wellington boots, with hair the colour of molten copper and eyes that were blazing me to oblivion, and all I could think was I wanted you.'

'You had a funny way of showing it,' she said weakly, and he gave a harsh bark of a laugh.

'I'm a funny man, Candy. You might find you've taken on more than you can chew.' She shook her head in denial, her face loving, and he smiled sardonically.

'When I found out who you were I couldn't believe it at first. It was as though fate had done me the ultimate dirty deal. I could see you didn't know the true facts about Michelle, but, even forgetting that, you seemed to detest the very ground I walked on.'

'I told you,' she said quickly, 'I was fighting myself as much as you and——'

'It's my turn now.' He touched her mouth with one warning finger and then traced her lips with his eyes. 'I never had any intention of closing the school down, Candy, but it was the only way I could think of to keep you coming back for more. Cruel, maybe, but you left me no choice, and I was desperate. Man, was I desperate. You were so proud, so fierce, so loyal to Michelle. I could hardly believe you were her sister; you're the very antithesis of her, you know. You're everything I'd tried to convince myself all those years ago Michelle was, closing my eyes to the things that didn't add up like the fool I was in those days.' He turned away to look through the windscreen, his mouth grim. 'When she told me that night that I'd been played for the biggest sucker since time began I wasn't totally surprised. There had always been a hardness, a

falseness . . .' He looked at her tightly. 'Beside
you, even at twelve, with your hair like a loo
brush, she was just a garishly painted doll.'

'Cam ——'

'And the others.' He moved his head in vi-
olent self-contempt. 'You wouldn't have liked
me in those days, Candy. I was trying to convince myself that I didn't need love, that it
was just an illusion, something in the minds
of weak people who needed a crutch. Those
women were just a momentary ease of frustration and then . . . nothing. I used them and
then I discarded them. Not very pretty, is it?'
he asked grimly. 'But that's how it was. The
only thing I can say in my defence is that each
of them knew the score.' He shrugged as he
glanced at her watching face. 'Life won't be
a bed of roses with me, Candy. I know I'm a
difficult man to live with, but if you want me
then I can promise you one thing: I'll never
look at another woman as long as I live. This
is your last chance to cut your losses and run.
Do you still say you love me?'

'More than life.' As she looked at him his
whole face and body seemed to lighten as

though a great weight had been lifted from his shoulders.

'Say that again,' he said huskily, 'and again and again...' And then she was in his arms, pressed close to his heartbeat, the warm, tantalising male smell of him filling her nostrils and seeping into the very pores of her skin until she felt she could drown in the touch and feel of him.

'I love you, carrot-tops...' His kisses were sending her liquid with a mixture of blazing desire and overwhelming relief that he had admitted it at last, his warm, firm hands on her body sending flickering sensual waves of delight right down to her toes. 'I shall love you every day of your life until you can't think, can't feel, can't know anything in the world except me.'

She was shaking uncontrollably when at last he raised his head, her clothing dishevelled and her silky hair spread out in glorious, ruffled disarray, a red, gleaming mass framing her flushed, hot face.

'How soon will you marry me?' he asked softly, a look of fierce triumph on his dark face at her utter, helpless capitulation.

'As soon as we can,' she whispered tremblingly. 'We can get one of those special licence things, can't we?'

'Don't you want a white wedding with bridesmaids and flowers and all the women crying?' He was nibbling at her ear between words and she moaned softly in reply. 'They'll all expect it in the village, you know. It's only fitting for the "squire's" wife.'

He was teasing her, but the import of his words suddenly reached through the sensual daze and she sat up suddenly, her eyes wide. 'The village? But I thought you wanted to live in Australia? You're selling the house and——'

'We'll be living in England,' he said firmly. 'I can't take you away from the village, but maybe a world cruise for our honeymoon, with a few months showing you off properly in Australia?'

'Anything you say,' she said weakly as his hands continued to work their magic, 'but no white wedding. I just want to be your wife. No fuss, no bother, just us, and maybe Mum and Dad. And I'm serious about the special licence. I've waited long enough for you, Cameron Strythe; I'm not about to let you change your mind.'

'Likewise, Miss Baker.' His hands were tracing the curve of her breasts and her breathing was ragged. 'You know, I could give your sister a big kiss right now,' he added wickedly, smiling in satisfaction as she reared up in protest.

'You could?' She glared at him. 'Well, isn't that nice!'

'But I thought you wanted me to forgive her, sweetheart?' he asked in mock surprise.

'Forgiving her is one thing; kissing her is another,' she said tartly. 'You try anything like that and you'll find out what it's like to come into contact with a saucepan. Anyway, she did betray you, after all. I'm not sure I can forgive her the hurt she caused.'

'You can, you have,' he whispered lovingly, 'and it was a sweet betrayal.' He touched the edge of her mouth with tiny, pulsating kisses. 'It's given me you, after all.'

She tried to reply, but his hands and mouth were growing more insistent and she couldn't think any more. A slow, luscious, rich ache was beginning to take charge of her body, and it suddenly made words wonderfully and deliciously unimportant.

MILLS & BOON NOW PUBLISH
EIGHT LARGE PRINT TITLES A MONTH.
THESE ARE THE EIGHT NEW TITLES
FOR DECEMBER 1993

———————— * ————————

SWEET BETRAYAL
by Helen Brooks

TOWER OF SHADOWS
by Sara Craven

THE UNMARRIED BRIDE
by Emma Goldrick

COUNTERFEIT LOVE
by Stephanie Howard

SIMPLY IRRESISTIBLE
by Miranda Lee

HUNTER'S MOON
by Carole Mortimer

AT ODDS WITH LOVE
by Betty Neels

A TEMPORARY AFFAIR
by Kate Proctor

MILLS & BOON NOW PUBLISH
EIGHT LARGE PRINT TITLES A MONTH.
THESE ARE THE EIGHT NEW TITLES
FOR JANUARY 1994

———————— * ————————

AN OLD ENCHANTMENT
by Amanda Browning

TRAVELLING LIGHT
by Sandra Field

LOVE WITHOUT REASON
by Alison Fraser

STRANGERS BY DAY
by Vanessa Grant

FIRE IN THE BLOOD
by Charlotte Lamb

GIVE A MAN A BAD NAME
by Roberta Leigh

FIERY ATTRACTION
by Emma Richmond

A HEALING FIRE
by Patricia Wilson